The Snake Oil Wars

The Snake Oil Wars

or

Scheherazade Ginsberg Strikes Again

PARKE GODWIN

A FOUNDATION BOOK

DOUBLEDAY

New York · London · Toronto · Sydney · Auckland

A Foundation Book
Published by Doubleday, a division of Bantam Doubleday Dell Publishing Group, Inc.
666 Fifth Avenue, New York, New York 10103

Doubleday, Foundation, and the portrayal of the letter F are trademarks of Doubleday,
a division of Bantam Doubleday Dell Publishing Group, Inc.

ISBN 0-385-24772-9

To those lucid and courageous minds who gave you the Inquisition, the Salem witch trials, Falwell, Robertson and the God-inspired Rule of the Righteous. To those intrepid souls who fight with unflagging zeal to remove from libraries dangerous books they have not read and from theaters those spiritually toxic films they have not seen, believing that thought is a controlled substance and secular thinking hazardous to mental health.

Prologue: Godhead,
or doing hard time

A few million years ago aliens invaded Earth.

Well, not really an invasion, just a class of graduating students who thought the young planet would be a fun place to party. Even more fun was leaving two annoying brothers, Barion and Coyul, stranded on this uncharted world where the highest form of life was a dismally unpromising ape. Everyone knew humanoid apes were losers that began primitive and violent, ended religious and lethal.

When the party got home, no one could remember exactly where they'd left the brothers. Not to worry. Being close to immortal, someone would find them sooner or later.

With nothing else to occupy their time, Barion and Coyul took a dead-ending ape and boosted its intelligence far earlier than was legal or even prudent. Though briefly fashionable, anthropoids were never a major study among their kind. The field work was spotty and accepted theories disastrously inaccurate.

For example, the post-life energy pools. These carbon cycle creatures continued after death as personal energy. As time went on, Barion and Coyul had to take charge of a growing mass of restless human personalities whom death rendered more permanent than improved—vicious, vain and self-deluding as ever. They polarized according to taste around Barion or Coyul, conditioned to expect an uppercase god, devil or other deities. To their pleasure or consternation, they found only the unassuming Barion in a place/state of mind called Topside, or an equally bewildering Below Stairs where Coyul ran his office like a salon and tried amid constant and colorful interruptions to compose music and keep his guests from each other's throats.

By the time Sorlij found the beleaguered brothers he'd marooned as a student prank, their experimental ape had evolved into a formidable creature whose emotions lagged far behind his intellect, capable of brilliance and mayhem in consecutive breaths.

Coyul, known by then as the Prince to his intimates, was left to clean up the mess and reeducate the results of their irresponsible meddling. Barion was taken home for trial and sentence.

EXTRACT FROM THE TRIAL OF BARION
UNAUTHORIZED EXPERIMENTATION AND
PREMATURE SEEDING
(From Sorlij's testimony)

SORLIJ: Against all reasonable projection, the species is promising but painfully immature. Fortunately their system is so remote, they won't constitute a danger to the main civilizations during those millennia needed to fit them for society at large.

Why was Coyul left rather than Barion?

SORLIJ: He did the crucial work in lifting the species over Cultural Threshold. I wouldn't have thought him capable of that, but he seems to know them better.

And your instructions to Coyul?

SORLIJ: The obvious: to bring their emotional growth into parity with their intellectual capacity. Some are already admirable specimens. But he must educate them away from dualistic or miraculous doctrines immediately.

Sorlij, are we to understand you blithely told him to negate the major religions of a species never without them anywhere in the known universe?

SORLIJ: The situation was tertiary. Their technology is already probing into space, yet their essential thinking hasn't changed in thousands of years, and these emotional tendencies are at the root of it like a large tumor in the base of the brain. Radical surgery was required.

Your own discipline is . . . ?

SORLIJ: Marine biology. My work is known throughout the field.

BARION: We always said he did a mean oyster.

Strike that remark from the record. Sorlij, given the parameters of this improbable anthropoid, do you as a scientist think they will accept Coyul's adjustment?

SORLIJ: Oh yes, eventually. What else can happen when you introduce an intelligent being to an empirical fact?

BARION: Among humans, civil war.

Strike that. Barion, you've already been warned about these impertinent interruptions.

BARION: Not impertinent but expert. I spent five million years among them. Anyway, what have I got to lose? I know I'm going to the Rock. I'm more worried about Coyul when he tries to educate Topside.

SORLIJ: Why? They can't destroy him.

BARION: They're human, they'll try. Hope springs eternal.

Your teeth are okay
but your gums have to come out

The television commentator's voice was far more familiar to older view-ers than his image on camera, cadenced and thoughtful, recalled as filtering through the shortwave radio static of 1940.

"This is John McBain for Topside Television. Not since the days of the London Blitz have I reported a story so fraught with consequence for Mankind. In a few moments, here in this Megachurch, Coyul, the alleged younger brother of Barion, will address the population of Top-side on an issue that promises to rock the establishment to its religious foundations. Barion was said by some to be God—not as we conceived of Him, but in fact. Darker stories are told of Coyul and his longtime sway over Below Stairs. One thing is certain: there are few Topside today not watching and listening for what Coyul has to say . . ."

McBain's estimate was conservative; there were few Below Stairs not watching with equal concern. Their friend and cosmic therapist, the beloved and sympatico Prince was assuming the mantle dropped by Barion. They knew Coyul's message to Topside would be as popular as the repeal of Prohibition to bootleggers.

Brooding in the cool, dark Sports Bar in the high-rise district of Below Stairs, Arnold Rothstein squinted at the TV set and wished money were still meaningful. In life he'd financed much of the action along Broadway, immortalized by Damon Runyon as the Brain. Now he felt ancient stirrings like a hunting call. He wanted to lay a sound bet for a piece of the action, however meaningless. The Brain turned to his drinking companion, a former New York editor who had offed himself through a fondness for chic narcotics.

"Ten to one they don't buy him at all. Seven to five they don't let him finish the telecast. Even money he won't make it out of the starting gate."

"I'll take some of that." The editor was known in betting circles as more of a fish than a handicapper. "The Prince is upscale, man. High concept, great moves. What's the bet?"

Arnold Rothstein considered. Money was a pleasant memory. The stake should be something one desired very much or wanted, out of common sense, to avoid. "Loser goes Topside to a revival meeting."

"That is a downer."

"I am not finished." Rothstein lifted a qualifying finger. "Just to make it interesting, loser has to come forward and wave to the winner on camera."

"What the hell, I feel lucky today. Bet." They shook hands. "Coyul will finesse the whole scene."

RIOT IN TOPSIDE MEGACHURCH!
FUNDYS VOTE RIOTOUS NO ON COYUL
NEW PREXY HAS NARROW ESCAPE

"This is Cathy Cataton for TSTV. Here's what's happening . . ."

Cathy Cataton didn't have the standard bland-blond screen image of Nancy Noncommit of BSTV, rather what some males would call a hatchet face: wide cheekbones and a narrow chin, her hair in short, dark curls. Only after death did she find her true calling as a newswoman.

"Coyul, the new appointee head of Topside triggered a riot in our largest Megachurch today when he attempted to set the record straight on his intended program. TSTV cameras were on the scene."

For Topside watchers who had never met or seen Coyul, his televised image was an anticlimax. He was short and plump, and in his mild, patient manner, there was a disconcerting cosmic ennui.

"Ladies and gentlemen—by whatever name, image or reputation you may know me—my name is Coyul. My brother Barion, who managed this establishment for so long, never represented himself as a god, never promised you a messiah, only wisdom and common sense to those rare spirits brave enough to heed it."

End of clip. Cataton again: "Coyul never got a chance to finish his presentation. He was interrupted by an American from Kansas."

And cut to Coyul again on the podium. "Barion found it necessary with so many conflicting faiths, to establish an absolute freedom of belief. Frankly, it never occurred to either of us to do otherwise from the time we started with you five million years ago—"

"Did Barion lie to us?"

Now the screen image was much more photogenic: a slender thirtyish man who ran agitated fingers through his rumpled hair. "I think every Christian is asking that question with me." A caption superimposed on the impassioned young image: LANCE CANDOR, AMERICAN. DIED SAVING THE PRESIDENT OF THE U.S. FROM ASSASSINATION. In the row behind Candor, a small woman in a faded paisley dress waved a placard:

KANSAS FOR GOD AND THE BIBLE!

In his vulnerable honesty, Lance Candor reminded viewers of young James Stewart, game but about to collapse on the Senate floor in the Capra movie. For American idealism, Candor made Stewart look like a Chicano.

Mr. Candor repeated his challenge: "Did Barion lie to us on the inerrancy of the Bible?"

And cut to Cathy Cataton again: "Candor was only the beginning. The riot broke out in earnest when Coyul matter-of-factly explained, or tried to explain, the essential fact of what he termed an anthropological experiment gone wrong—"

Coyul again, visibly aware of laboring in a lost cause. "You're not finished. Not nearly finished. You're not the center of a flattering myth, but let me help you."

"KILLLLL HIMMMM—"

The cameras caught a forward surge through the audience, like tall grass lashed by a high wind. Acres of people rising, stampeding down on the mild little figure in front of the microphones. The tidal wave of moral outrage converged on the podium, engulfing Coyul as he simply vanished and Cataton's voice-over ended the segment. " 'Trouble right here in River City.' The confrontation brewing for years between radical and conservative religious viewpoints here in Topside seems to have come to a head in Coyul, thought by many to be the Devil. How long his authority will be accepted, if at all, is up for guesses."

Below Stairs in the Sports Bar, the New York editor tried to hedge his lost bet with Arnold Rothstein. "Okay, I go Topside. All the way across that dead-ass Void. But no getting Born Again; that's not part of the bet."

The Brain was a gracious winner. "Just so I can see you on camera."

"Hey, Mr. Rothstein." Legs the bartender turned up the TV sound, still tuned to Cathy Cataton. "Get this."

". . . repeat the last item just in. A few minutes ago, Lance Candor, who challenged Coyul in the Megachurch, hurled a bomb into Coyul's office—"

Rothstein's lip curled. "And they call this hell."

"—completely destroying the new appointee's salon, Coyul himself and two guests. Candor has not yet been apprehended and Fundamentalists throughout Topside are cheering his action."

The Brain turned to his drinking companion. "Do I win or do I win?"

"Yeah, yeah." The vanquished editor communed with the bottom of his glass. "Beats me how you could call it so close."

"Son," said the wise old Brain, "it is a lead pipe cinch you do not hail from Kansas." He tapped his empty glass on the bar. "Legs? One more time, no ice."

■ 2 ■

Hazards of terminal patriotism;
enter a blonde

Coyul didn't expect to be blown up. After his fiasco in the Megachurch, he looked forward to a restful interlude in his salon, with Richard Wagner the morning's only scheduled appointment. Coyul would rather discuss music than theology any day, and Wagner needed approval for a new operatic extravaganza. Approaching his salon, he heard the mellow tones of his piano in a very un-Wagnerian strain. He opened the door: an oasis to the jaded eye.

Barion never did much by way of furniture: ancient file cabinets, a plain desk, a few wooden chairs. Coyul's sense of decor was more opulent. White walls, subtle lighting, furnishings in cream and beige leather. There was a liquor cabinet for guests whose virtues clung beyond death, several music stands, spacious cathedral windows through which the view changed to the watcher's whim. To one side stood Coyul's computer for musical notation. The white grand piano dominated the salon.

As he suspected, not the Giant of Bayreuth at the piano but George Gershwin, fat cigar clamped between his teeth, long fingers caressing melody from the keyboard.

"George, good to see you." Coyul brightened immediately. "Is that from the new show?"

"The love song for the second act. Want to hear the lyrics?"

"Do I want a migraine?" The crisp, staccato voice came from the depths of an easy chair turned toward the windows. Aloof as Gershwin was convivial, George Kaufman rose in ectomorphic sections, left arm coiled around his neck to scratch at his right ear. He gazed gloomily out the window on a privately remembered view of Forty-fourth Street in New York. "How was your opening, Prince?"

Coyul sank down on the leather lounge. "Don't wait up for the reviews. Told them the truth and started a riot."

"We heard of some disagreement," Gershwin said.

"What else is new?" Kaufman scrutinized the rug at his feet, bending to remove a tiny piece of lint which he deposited in an ashtray. "They've been shooting without a script for years."

"I was expecting Wagner—not keenly, but have you seen him?"

"Oh, he came." Gershwin flirted with the Magic Fire theme, turning the phrase subtly blue. "Took one look at us and left."

"Well, I deserved one break today," Coyul said candidly. "To what do I owe this delightful recess? Problems with the show?"

"It's that refugee from Woodstock they gave me for a collaborator," Kaufman barked in his best curmudgeon voice. "Ricky Remsleep, the professional hippy. Wrote a love scene for the second act. No pace, no laughs, just soggy lines with *guitar* music yet. Every time Remsleep feels significant, he wants a guitar behind the actors." The co-author of memorable Broadway hits scowled at the rug. "I hate love scenes."

"The act needs a love scene," Gershwin appealed to Coyul, "and the scene needs a song, and your office was a good place to argue."

Kaufman found another microscopic piece of lint on the carpet. He wandered back to the window, digging in his ear. "Groucho could add five minutes to an act with ad libs, but at least he got laughs."

Coyul passed a hand over the coffee table; a sumptuous spread of *hors d'oeuvres* appeared in its wake. Kaufman was no more interested in food dead than he had been alive, but post life had cured Gershwin of composer's stomach. He loaded a plate and carried it back to the piano. "Who started the riot?"

"Fundamentalists, wouldn't you know; very big in America now. 'Age cannot wither nor custom stale.' Play me the love song, George."

Like most Gershwin songs, the limpid, deceptively simple melody would be remembered long after the show. Coyul sipped Glen Morangie and allowed his mind to wander with the music. Five million years among humans, from Pithecanthropus to George Bush, could jaundice even an acting god. Coyul surrendered to nostalgia, longing for his own mercurial kind. Where was Barion now? Where was Purji, charming, truant and irresponsible as an explosion herself?

The yearning in Coyul was rare but genuine. Odder still, he'd thought of Purji often lately, as if her energy were actually coming nearer. No hope there: the last anyone heard of that splendid female, she'd dropped out of society altogether. Disappeared.

Gershwin modulated into an arresting key change. "Here's the bridge."

The unmusical Kaufman suffered. "George, couldn't you just mail it in?"

"Gonna make all the difference. Get this, Coyul."

"Get *this,* Devil!"

Coyul had only a split second to see Lance Candor poised in the doorway, the hissing satchel charge in his hand. "You're dealing with Americans, Satan!" Lance hurled the bomb. "Take that!"

Startled, Coyul could only view the trajectory of the missile—up, over, down between smoked salmon and caviar—and hear Lance's yell of triumph as he darted away. The explosion was spectacular. Coyul, Kaufman, Gershwin, the piano and *hors d'oeuvres* whirled together in a Cuisinart effect, blossomed outward in a spray and splattered against the broken walls. Heavier objects did not travel so far. Gershwin's head found itself nose down among the shards of a Waterford bowl. Nearby, Kaufman's equally dissociated head fixed him with a dyspeptic scowl.

"What did I tell you? That song is a bomb."

One of the benefits of post life was the convenience of ordering your own scenery according to mood. Richard Wagner, composer of *Das Ring,* paced through a breathtaking landscape of Bavarian mountains and primeval forest. Part of his mind sketched at the newly conceived musical dramas. The rest occupied itself with loathing Coyul. *Herr* Wagner was an accomplished loather, but fair about it. He'd always given equal time to Barion.

The trouble began long ago when Verdi praised Wagner to Coyul, saying, "His genius is infinite."

"His vulgarity perhaps," Coyul differed. "His genius is wholly confined to music."

The remark got back to Wagner, and Coyul was thereafter an object of Wagnerian detestation. However, some permission would be required for the new opera cycle since casting would involve thousands. Wagner was grateful to have missed Coyul when he called. Another time perhaps. He might even petition by mail.

The new work would be a series of opera about the Aryan invasion of India. Hitler loved the concept, and his taste was impeccable. Wagner envisioned the penultimate scene of the first opera: thousands of tall blond warriors descending through the clouds upon a stunned and churlishly ungrateful rabble of dwarfish *lumpen.* The heroic vanguard would include his heroine who would enter lost, pursued by a horde of stunted, slavering villains. There would be a nimbus of light about her golden head, a beacon to the Aryan hero who rescued and joined her in a twenty-minute duet. She must have a name whose sound was beauty itself. Statuesque as her conquering kind, his heroine would be—

Would be . . .

Richard Wagner halted and stared.

Not would be. Was. There. Redundant as breathing might be, Wagner gasped aloud. Directly in his path, lounging against a centuried oak, was his creation incarnate. Cascades of hair like molten gold fell over creamy shoulders so white there seemed a bluish undertint. A truly legendary figure was barely covered by a brief, diaphanous costume that would have caused riots at Bayreuth. She was at least eight feet tall, ninety-six utterly flawless inches. Not Germanic, more striking than Amazon. For her height, not an inch or an ounce was too little, too much or misplaced. Wagner flushed with ardor. Flagstad and Nilsson were forgotten. Never until this moment had his artistic intent been so perfectly realized in flesh. Her leitmotif, fresh as the first dawn in Valhalla, flooded through his soul in a spontaneous burst of creation. He could hear it, see it finished in score for two hundred instruments—

Her Viking-blue eyes wide with curiosity, the dazzling behemoth bent to examine a fallen leaf. The flow of her body through the simple movement was sensuality itself. She caught sight of Wagner—"Oh!"—and focused on him with the fascination of novelty and a smile that put all his remembered hormones on red alert.

You are Brunhilde, he adored.

"No, my name is Purji. I've only just arrived." She appeared to understand him telepathically; Wagner heard her in German. "What an athletic tongue you think in. Here, sit down and help me get my bearings."

She took his hand. Wagner was wafted swiftly upward to a thick limb of the oak. Next to the leviathan Purji he felt like a ventriloquist's dummy. "There now." She gazed around in surmise. "From the fascinating but unstable nature of my surroundings, I've landed in a post-life energy pool." She stroked Wagner like a lapdog. "You are a dear little thing."

"And you . . . are a goddess?"

She nodded. "Used to be. Among the Keljians. Pardon me. I'm so used to their proportions." Her fabulous image dissolved, shrank and recombined to the same perfection on a smaller scale. "I'm looking for a dear friend who *must* be somewhere hereabouts. Coyul, a lovely male like yourself."

"Coyul?" Wagner's ego bristled. No more was she perfection's glass. She even spoke with Coyul's clipped *auslander* accent. "You are a friend of that spiritual gargoyle?"

"I *am* in the right place," Purji bubbled. "More than friends. I've been in love with him since school. Eons in your time."

"There is no accounting for passion."

"Well, consistency at least. Passion is only a moment, but—" The rest of Purji's sentiment was lost in a yelp of surprise as a tremendous detonation rocked their tree and tumbled them from the limb to the ground. From somewhere beyond Wagner's *schwarzwald,* brownish smoke rose in an ominous plume from unseen destruction. The retired goddess appeared more vindicated than alarmed.

"I see you have an advanced concept of politics. Would you be a kind gentleman and direct me to Coyul?"

Shaken, Wagner did not attempt to get up, merely waved Purji toward the rising mushroom of smoke. "That way, *fräulein.* Just follow the debris."

■ 3 ■

Downturns in the deity line

Purji read Coyul's unmistakable energy very near but weak. Finding him would be a problem. The remnants of the salon were unpleasantly fluid, vacillating queasily between matter and energy. The destruction reminded Purji of holy wars on Keljia. Walls, furniture and smaller objects were rubbled together in an architectural salad dressed with a blackish-pink substance she would rather not dwell on.

"My poor Coyul."

From somewhere nearby, a woozy voice responded, "Uh . . . yes?"

"Coyul?" Purji cast about anxiously. "Where are you?"

"Sort of all over. Could you sift around a bit?"

Purji found him in installments, this bit pureed over a section of wall, that scattered on the floor, torso neatly processed through up-ended piano strings in the egalitarian manner of an egg slicer. Under a light fall of first edition pages from a splintered bookcase, Purji discovered Coyul's head. "Darling!"

"Purji." The mild blue eyes peered at her foggily, trying to focus. "I felt you near, couldn't think how. George? Hello?"

"Who, dear?"

"Innocent bystanders. Hello, Georges plural, G and K? Are you there? Purji, do you see anything that might belong to two tall men?"

"No. Everything I've found so far seems to go with you." Tenderly she wiped the Camembert from his bruised brow—difficult, as his head kept melting to soft, grayish Jell-O. "What an awful—have I come at a bad time?"

"You? Never," the head assured her, "but you're not catching me at my best."

"I thought for a moment that ghastly mess on the walls—"

"Farewell the salmon and caviar." Coyul gathered himself for the effort. "This will be difficult." His mind, stunned and reeling inside a human cranium, couldn't do anything right at first. He managed a form that might have been rendered by a child with a blunt crayon, but the results kept melting to a mish-mash of flickering light and gelatinous matter. For a moment he realized an eerie resemblance to John Kennedy but couldn't hold it.

"Closer," Purji encouraged. "Keep going."

"Keep talking," he moaned. "All I hear is a dull bong."

With a clearing mind, Coyul gradually reconstituted himself. A golden blob resolved to his favorite lamé dressing gown and filled out with familiar proportions. Amorphous features resolved to character and expression. Pallid, shaken, but restored—something like Dylan Thomas in his later years—Coyul sat up and smiled at Purji.

"There's my darling."

"Purji! It's been eons. Where's your ship?"

"Out there in matter phase." She gestured blithely between kisses.

"Let me *look* at you." Definitely worth the effort, still bleary as his sight was. Beside Purji's idealized Keljian form, the best Miss Universe was a victim of birth defect. One might imagine the sensuality of a Joan Collins superimposed on Mariel Hemingway and the result raised to the tenth power of femininity. In a swaddling choir robe and with a Bible in her hand, Purji would still be outlawed in most American states.

"Dazzling as ever, you erotic triumph," Coyul vowed. "I last saw you—when?"

The memory was dear to Purji, undimmed by eons. "At home, the radical students' demonstration, remember? All of us showing off, making love in human form, and so bad at it."

"Like polar bears in a Charleston contest," Coyul recalled. "But what fun it was."

"Darling." Purji kissed him again with sharpening intent and therapeutic effect. "It still is."

After impromptu love amid the ruins, Coyul felt more like his old self, restoring the salon to former glory and setting out caviar and smoked salmon for Purji. "A delicious human innovation, one of their better efforts. Try some."

She nibbled tentatively. "Looked so visceral on the walls."

After a quick search, Coyul had decided not to worry about Gershwin or Kaufman. They'd probably recombined on their own and gone home. Gershwin would take it in stride, but the hypochondriac Kaufman might let it ruin his week.

"Now, Purji, where in the universe have you been?"

"Oh, simply everywhere." Draped over the lounge, Purji was delightfully discovering scotch. "Chasing the stars in their courses."

"You just vanished."

"So did you. Of course there is a vast difference between being marooned with monkeys"—she punctuated her thought with a wave of her glass and a small hiccup—"and being taken up socially by Keljian humans."

Though larger than Earthers and utterly beautiful, Keljians were still meandering through a Bronze Age state of development, but for Purji the interlude had been glorious. "You are in the presence of the most popular fertility goddess Keljia ever knew."

"No! You theological brigand."

Purji searched Coyul's mind like a memory bank for a comparable image. "I was a star, an unqualified hit. They were sacrificing to me day and night."

"Ye gods, not people?"

"Anyone they could throw and tie. You know humans when they get carried away. I discouraged the practice immediately, willed the fires to go out. Instead of combusting to my glory, the sacrifice lay there complaining until they finally got the point and just sent flowers. Oh, but it was lovely when they chose my annual consort." Purji lay back with a blissful sigh. "Keljian males are admirable. Picture it, dear: thousands of years of celebrity, festivals, done by the best sculptors, invoked in love songs. But then . . . oh, then."

"What happened? Wait, let me guess. Monotheism."

Purji dissolved from the lounge to reappear in somber gray near a window, a tragic figure. "My beloved Keljians. No plumbing but pain-fully religious. Monotheism it was. In came the patriarchs and virtually invented guilt. They created a male deity grim as death, somewhere between an articulate volcano and a psychotic child. I should have seen it coming."

"Indeed you should have, at your age."

She frowned at him. "That is a boorish remark. I am younger than you."

"I do have a little job experience." Coyul easily pictured her decline. In time her worship became unpopular, then persecuted. Political power identified with the male godhead and found it pious as well as profitable to flay the old order with a vengeance.

"Life became grotesque," Purji lamented. "There I was, demoted to a sleazy demon with the nastiest motives and character ascribed to me, exorcised every other week, I was *exhausted*. Finally I threw fame to the winds and caught the next survey ship home. Now it's happening to you. Coyul"—she brimmed suddenly with mischievous inspiration—"why don't we just take my ship and find some ordinary little world, nothing elaborate, and be gods together?"

The notion of a cozy little mom-and-pop religion was briefly tempt-ing. "No, I can't. Barion's on the Rock and it's my fault as much as his these high-tech Comanches have become what they are. I've got to help them grow up. All suggestions gratefully accepted."

Someone coughed politely in the entrance. Three distinguished older men waited discreetly to be noticed: an archbishop in full canonicals, a tall man in Victorian garb and a smaller man who would have stood out as an American anywhere. Coyul bounced up to greet them.

"Gentlemen, please come in. This is Purji, a lady of my own race. Purji, let me present—"

"Considering our mission, we would prefer to remain anonymous for the time," the bearded Victorian gentleman interjected with a bow to Purji. "Madam."

"It's about Candor," the American said.

"I see. Then, Purji, let me present three gentlemen from"—Coyul ticked them off—"Westminster, Canterbury and Washington."

"Delighted." The archbishop inclined his mitered head to Purji. "Candor indeed is our argument. My king would have had his head at Tyburn by sundown."

"Young Mr. Candor, dashing as a trenchcoat and nearly as bright. I really haven't decided what action to take," Coyul told them. "Perhaps you can advise me."

The delegation exchanged glances, electing the Prime Minister to speak first. "The press is already taking sides, making an issue. Your inaugural appearance did not find a receptive audience."

"To put it mildly."

"Shall I address you as Prince?"

"If you will, or simply Coyul. Barion never stood on ceremony, neither will I."

"Prince." The P.M. had a long habit of deference to royalty under a single-minded queen who demanded it. "Every responsible citizen Topside is shocked and revolted by Candor's action."

"And the rest are cheering him," the American rasped in his gravelly voice. "Son, you've got a bad situation here. I never saw anything firm up so fast."

"Fanaticism is not too strong a term," said the grave P.M.

The American's input was far pithier. "Arrest Candor. Make an example. The Fundys and fringe lunatics will be all over television with their side, making that little cockroach into Christ. There's got to be a strong commonsense position to fight them."

"Frankly, gentlemen, I've never arrested anyone before," Coyul considered. "What crime and what charge? This is post life, not Earth. Mayhem dwindles to an emotional snit."

"Not to *them*. Look, Coyul." The American made his points as he had in life, forcefully, both hands up, edges forward, cutting decisively through problems. "You know I've faced my share of bullies and bullshit, from Klansmen to generals with a goddamned Caesar complex. Candor's not important, but he's sure as hell dangerous. That dim-bulb S.O.B. loves being a hero. Did y'see him on TV the day he was shot? He did everything but lick the camera when he went down. And his trial is going to be standing room only with hardshells who define freedom as their right to tell you how to think. Indict his grandstanding ass, pardon my French, convict him and ship him Below Stairs. The little bastard will love suffering long's someone takes pictures."

The P.M. cleared his throat. "If I may? Her Majesty and Prince Albert agree that a strong and immediate showing must be made for the conservative cause."

"Thank you," Coyul acknowledged. "They would not receive me when I called."

"Her Majesty conveyed no disapproval," the archbishop hastened to clarify, "neither did any former English ruler. Merely that until your position is more clearly defined, reception might be misconstrued."

"I quite understand."

"On your authority, Prince," the P.M. pressed, "my provosts are ready to arrest Lance Candor."

Coyul picked out random notes on the piano in time with his thoughts. "I don't know what to tell you. The only assassin I ever liked was Wilksey Booth, but still . . ."

Purji's suggestion was wifely and sensible. "You've had a grisly morning, dear. Why not sleep on the question? A nap would be just the thing."

"Thank you, Purji. True, gentlemen, I'm not as young as I used to be. I've seen all this before and will again before your kind grows up or blows up. Purji and I are of an ancient race, one of the earliest. We found ourselves virtually alone in the young universe. Perhaps it was loneliness that sent us out looking for someone to think back at us. Not always rewarding where humans are concerned. Except for the blood and misery, your history is bad Gilbert and Sullivan, and democracy, I'm afraid, a lovely illusion."

"So is Father Christmas," the P.M. observed with warm wisdom. "For all of that, I shall still read my Dickens each Christmas Eve and hang my stocking on the mantel. December would be barren without it."

"Unpopular decisions are always rough," the American reminded Coyul from direct experience. "Hard to make, hard to live with."

"Yes." Coyul read too many remembered nightmares in the man from Missouri. "Yours were more difficult. For the thousands dead, remember the million saved."

"I try, Coyul. Every day."

"I guess that's what it amounts to. Thank you, Harry. And you, P.M. I'll still hang up my stocking." Coyul closed the piano. "Arrest the swashbuckling Candor."

The P.M. bowed formally and turned to the entrance. "Sar-major!"

Into Coyul's salon marched two impressively muscular British sergeants, vintage 1870, stamping to rigid attention before the Prime Minister. "SAH!"

"Carry out your instructions."

"SAH!" A whip-crack salute. "Left turn! Quick-HAHH! One-two-one-two—"

The posse and all to follow were now in motion. The delegation withdrew. Coyul sat down. For a moment his face was shadowed by all of his long ages. "Five million years, Purji. See how it goes?"

"Poor darling. You won't have a moment for your music. Take your nap."

4

Children of the century

TOPSIDE AROUSED BY BOMBING!
CONSERVATIVES SHAKEN. FUNDYS CLOSE RANKS
BEHIND CANDOR
CANDOR INDICTED. WIFE VOWS
TO STAND BY HIM

Lance's television was state of the heart, working on simple thought control. He willed it now to replay: there he was between two marshalls, leaving his arraignment, Letti hovering behind. As Lance passed out of shot, Letti turned to eyeball the TSTV cameras.

Destiny's second call. He was a hero again. In the coming trial, win or lose, he would be ranked with the martyrs. Lance watched the clip again, then willed the TV to run his funeral in Kansas. No matter how often he viewed the flag-draped casket, Letti brave beside it, Lance felt a lump in his throat and a deep satisfaction in the splendid closure to an American life not studded with prominence until its last, sufficing days.

He and Letti had been part of a Christian Reconstructionist delegation to Washington to realign the Constitution with Biblical precepts. Nothing in Lance's brief life had ever been so important. Obviously a nation constituted under God could *not* tolerate abortion, *must* reinstitute (Protestant) school prayer, *must* replace the teaching of evolution with creation science. The inerrancy of the Bible was urgently needed to replace ambiguous secular law. The Constitution was no longer adequate, if it ever had been; the ship of state was foundering. Lance admired the neatness of the phrase, especially since he thought it up himself.

"A tight ship for a leaky barge," he said at the Mayflower Hotel, pleased that even the suspiciously left-ish *Washington Post* quoted him.

His last, utterly fine days. Their delegation descending on the Capital, setting up in the Mayflower. The dinner rally in the big convention room with coverage by the major networks—and sure enough, when they checked the ten o'clock news, there he *was* at the rostrum.

Lance settled back and reran the rally clip. A shot from below as he stood behind the rostrum in his last one-for-the-gipper plea to the faithful before they met with their representatives in the House and Senate. The drama of the scene always thrilled Lance: himself, visibly tired but flushed with sincerity, running on energy, the hair falling boyishly over his forehead—

"We're building a tight ship in place of a leaky barge! The Constitution no longer reflects the word of God, and where it doesn't, it has to GO!"

Cheers.

They were cheering *him* for the first time since he'd won his eagle scout badge in Neosho Falls. That's all he wanted, not money. He lost time and money from his civil service job working for the church. Lost out on a promotion for taking so much time off, though Lance never grudged the effort. He wanted to give God back to the country. To the people. Just that, every now and then, Lance Candor wanted to stand in the warm light of destiny.

And it came to pass that God and destiny beamed on him.

Lance relaxed deeper into the French Provincial chair and plunked his feet up on the leather hassock before remembering that the hassock, like the large porcelain dogs flanking the never-lit fireplace, was Letti's pride. He put his feet down quickly. Now he called up the news film of his last day, last moments of life on Connecticut Avenue in the Capitol. The President stepped out of his limousine, smiling genially in the sunlight, waving to the crowd. The camera panned the press of spectators, passing over Lance and Letti.

"There we are, honey," Letti brayed from the living room arch. "Big's life'n twice as purty."

"Wait." Lance leaned forward, eager. "Here it comes."

A shot rang out, strangely flat on the soundtrack. The camera jerked back and forth across the crowd, then found the assassin, a reedy young man with mad eyes, brandishing a small automatic.

"Looky there," Letti hooted. "There's that li'l shitass sunvabetch! What's his name anyhow?"

"Herman J. Detweiler."

In the passion play of Lance's own immortality, Detweiler was a mere extra. Below Stairs, brooding over whisky for a lost love, Herman saw it differently: twenty-two, unemployed, and his girl friend had called him a useless wimp. Since he didn't like the President anyway, he could erase two bad impressions with one shot.

"This is the good part." Letti rattled the ice in her vodka and Coke. "Do it slow."

Fate unfroze and moved forward in slow motion. The gun came up in Herman's hand. An alert Secret Service guard reached for his own weapon, but not fast enough, not near fast enough and—

—then Lance Candor, slim interceptor, dove out of the crowd to shield the President with his own body. CLOSE-UP: Lance, mouth open and twisted with agony as the bullet thudded into him, crumpling slowly, frame by frame, to die at the President's feet. Accompanied in less than a second by the hapless Herman when the Secret Service blew him all over the sidewalk. His girlfriend wept demurely for the evening news, carefully underscored the fact that they hadn't dated much, mumbled about Herm's problems, and married a CPA. Below Stairs, Herman took up with a waitress who thought him dangerous and exciting.

About Herman's plot resolution, Lance knew or cared nothing; his own was marching onscreen with cadenced tread to glory. Interior of a white-walled church in Wichita: Lance's funeral, six honorary pall bearers from Fort Myer stalwart over the casket. Cut to the cemetery and the interment—and Letti *again* looking directly into the camera. "You always *do* that."

"Do what? Honest, honey, I just thought someone said something to me and I turned around to see who was it."

The thirty-inch screen filled now with a *Time* cover depicting Lance with lean cheeks and indomitable chin against a backdrop of the American flag.

LANCE CANDOR, AMERICAN

The end was worth an unhappy married life. Lately when Letti had stoned herself to sleep with vodka and Valium, Lance added a Mantovani soundtrack while his favorite movie queen undulated into shot, wickedly knowing and intent, to ravage him in delightful slow motion. Neither death nor glory had improved his sex life. Lance was as deprived in death as in life.

"Still a martyr," he sighed cryptically. "They'll be coming soon."

"Don't you fret," Letti soothed, straightening a picture over the plastic-covered couch. "House looks real nice and so will I, just give me a minute and make me a fresh drink while you're resting."

"I'll miss you so much," Lance yearned. "I mean why can't we go upstairs and—"

Letti headed him off at the pass with the skill of long practice. "I would but I got one of those headaches."

"You always have a headache. Even dead you have headaches?"

"Just I'm delicate and too much of a lady to complain." Letti fluttered a plump hand across her brow. "If they're coming, you don't want your wife looking tacky."

The burden of tack was a cross Letti bore beyond death. Her house was done only nominally in French Provincial, adulterated by a kind of Reader's Digest Awful. The print she straightened was a Keen moppet, large-eyed and lachrymose. Her pride, the porcelain hearth dogs, further diluted any purity of style. There were heart-shaped red pillows on her bed, a needlepoint sampler above the veneered headboard proclaiming: GOD IS LOVE.

God perhaps, but not Letti Candor.

Letti was on record as having learned her Bible at her daddy's knee. She learned more on his knee when her mother was absent. Daddy alternated between furtive molestations and bouts of guilt in Old Testament doses. He dramatized his redemptive mode by not shaving, which made him look more unkempt than patriarchal. Letti liked Lance all through school and during their chaste engagement, but always equated sex with Daddy fumbling under her clothes and making her uncomfortable. She never finked on him, but neither forgot nor forgave. Until her wedding day, Letti avoided sex on principle. Five hours after the ceremony, she found she disapproved because she didn't like it—especially with Lance, whose lovemaking was more spastic than effective.

Not that he got all that much practice. In the moment before he leaped in the path of the bullet, he was fantasizing about the likely young woman on Detweiler's right, nearest his gun arm—and died as he lived, unslaked. Through his years with Letti he pondered with no answer how a woman with shrieking relish and total recall for every dirty joke ever heard had so little interest in the real thing. In private Letti had a mouth like a Texas prison guard bullhorning through a riot. In public she wore a sunhat, prim white gloves, and got more Southern than usual. Lance always ascribed to inconsolable grief the fact that Letti died a week after he did; actually she dipped deeper than usual into the vodka and forgot how many sleeping pills she'd taken. There were no newsreels of her funeral, but she kept some of the flowers.

To be fair, Letti endured her own disabusements. Expecting to meet God immediately on death, she was puzzled by Barion and put off by his Yankee accent, flatly refused to accept Yeshua as her Jesus—"I mean, Bernice, he's so *Jewy*-lookin' "—and felt Saint Paul was not the sort she'd want to be seen with in nice places like Topeka or Wichita. She settled down in a pretty house with Lance. If Topside was not Heaven, there was still recompense. With imagination the only limit, Letti could "do" her house continually and at will. Her fancy ran barefoot through the Hereafter. She had a whole "suit" of rooms, one for dressing, one for lounging, a few extra for redecorating when inspiration struck. Bathrooms virtually expired in their deodorized, pink and blue, his-and-hers daintiness. In the (separate) chintz-choked bedrooms, blankets and spreads tucked tight enough for a Marine D.I. were forbidden Lance to nap on until he retired at night. Someone might come and see them messy.

Letti swept into her dressing room now as to a council on national crisis. There would sure as hell be news cameras with the officers come to get her Lance. The hero's lady would not be caught looking tacky. By iron rule, Letti never emerged from her dressing room without doing her morning makeup, nor from her house, God forbid, without doing it over. With a generous blob of cold cream, she now obliterated the morning's creation and began from scratch. Letti's scratch was unremarkable as a measured mile of Texas Panhandle. Daumier might have found it interesting. Letti Candor did not. As with her furniture, so her face: cover it pretty.

On her satin-skirted dressing table, her makeup awaited like munitions set out for battle, but Letti was a nearsighted cannoneer with the cosmetic touch of a stonemason. Her pallid coloring soon vanished under several layers of Ever After Tan #2, while cheekbones appeared in startling white to be dry-sponged into the overall illusion. Eyes might be the windows of the soul, but to Letti a bare window was an admission of neglect. No casement uncurtained, no eye unadorned. When finished, with huge DuPont lashes and dramatic liner for accent, Letti's eyes, marooned in the Sahara of her pancake, looked like two roaches crawling through a sandstorm. She had little regard for the difference between diffuse daylight and the mellow lights that bathed her TV idols. Indoors or out, Letti looked as if she'd been done by an apprentice mortician working in shadow.

Lance came into the dressing room to cup her breasts and nestle his cheek against her hair, his voice husky with need. "You are the prettiest thing in the world."

Letti wriggled with annoyance. "Lance, honey, you're gonna mess me up. Leave me be now, y'hear?"

He sat backward on the bench beside her, disconsolate and doom-ridden. "Just that they'll be coming soon, and I thought—" He tried to hug her. Letti writhed him off again.

"Now, Lance—"

"Aw please, Letti."

"Ah *told* you I have a headache. It's my period again."

"You can't get periods here."

Letti pouted into the mirror. "I got sympathetic pains."

"That's what I get when you're pregnant, which you never got. You mean phantom pains."

"Well, that's what I got."

Lance got up and wandered morosely to the chinz-curtained window. "You know how long it's been?"

Letti didn't, concentrating on her lip gloss. "Can't be but a couple weeks."

"Couple—Letti, it was last December."

"Well, that was for Christmas. You were so cute in your li'l red blazer. What you looking so sad about?"

"They're here. English soldiers again. You'd think at least they'd send Americans."

"Shit, I ain't even dressed." Letti flew between dressers, drawers and closet, snatching at clothes. The rap on the front door sounded H-hour. "Lay-ance! Zip me up, goddammit."

Lance complied with a sigh. "I don't want to be unfaithful to you, Letti."

"What?" The idea froze Letti in her tracks. Beneath layers of gloss, her kewpie-doll mouth quivered. "Lance Candor, that is the most un-Christian thing a husband ever said." She never wanted to sleep with him but refused to think of anyone else trying. Taking him away, leaving her alone. "You wouldn't do that, would you, honey?"

Lance had enough dramatic instinct to answer her with no more than an eloquent glance. Another rap on the door. He started downstairs.

"Shee-it, I hate to go out half done, feel so tacky." In the mirror Letti primped her brassy blond hair with nervous fingers, added her largest earrings and sunhat, snatched up a pair of white gloves—and descended like Gloria Swanson to her close-up.

◼ 5 ◼

Song of Scheherazade

". . . Cathy Cataton for TSTV news outside the Candor home where Lance Candor is about to be taken into custody for the bombing of Coyul's office. His forthcoming trial will be seen by many as more a referendum on Coyul's power than Candor's action. As you can see—"

On Coyul's screen, the TSTV camera panned over a crowd of several hundred, a forest of placards raised high:

> FREE LANCE CANDOR
> WE LOVE LANCE
> DOWN WITH COYUL
> CHRISTIANS WANT GOD, NOT EXPERIMENTS
> GOD FIRED SATAN ONCE. LET'S DO IT AGAIN

"—the emotional support for Candor is out in force and far more vocal than the opposition in what promises to be the Topside issue of the century. And here comes Lance Candor with his wife."

Observing the tragic Lance onscreen, Coyul wondered when humans would come up with a new script. He might have shrugged off the whole sad scene but for the job to be done and a sense of responsibility inconvenient as a hangnail. Barion started from ego but stayed to try with these creatures. He could do no less.

"Purji, stop gyrating and watch this. Saint Lance is about to be ingenuous for his public."

Learning Earth customs and language with the speed of an ambitious computer, Purji had just discovered the Charleston—airborne, long legs flying in syncopation. She vanished mid-kick and reappeared in his lap to nibble at his earlobe. "Take me, lover. Ravage me."

"Peace, you insatiable force of nature. Watch this."

"I don't want to watch a newsreel. The cartoons are better written."

Flanked by two massive guards, Lance looked painfully vulnerable and sincere. He swallowed, pushed the hair back from his forehead. "I —I just want to say that if I have to go to hell for what I've done, I'd do it again. Ten times over."

The crowd screamed their support, placards bobbing furiously. Now a shot of Letti: Purji became more interested. "Is that a tragic mask she's wearing?"

"Only her taste," Coyul said.

Letti—brave but fighting back tears: "Ah will stand by my husband in his hour of trial. And God *will* come to our aid."

"Visually fascinating," Purji mused. "So barbaric—AGHH!" She went indigo with shock as the moving camera presented barbarism beyond anything from the dark night of the Keljian stone age. Over several hundred million years and countless galaxies, Purji had never seen anything like the new apparition raging on the screen. In living color, WE LOVE LANCE placard on high over electric pink hair, the skinny young woman looked like a Bakshi creation done in one of Ralph's darkest moments. Her knobby-kneed, slightly bowed legs, encased in skintight leopard pants, teetered on platform shoes. Around her waist was draped a decorative brass cartridge belt.

"This is unique." Purji froze the classic image. The whatever-it-was petrified in mid-swing, placard raised like a battle ax ready to descend in mayhem. "Coyul, that *is* a female?"

He chuckled with recognition. "Scheherazade Ginsberg, a seething relic of the late sixties. Very radical chic."

Purji unfroze the action. History jerked forward with Scheherazade Ginsberg, tigress of revolution—

"Let him *go,* you fucking establishment PIG!"

Ms. Ginsberg swung her sign like a power hitter. WE LOVE LANCE broke over the head of a resentful British sergeant, now edited to WE LOVE. Scheherazade glared into the camera, challenging the home viewers of Topside.

"Lance is meaningful!" she screamed as police dragged her away. "He is *now.*"

A dungeon: dark, damp stone walls, a drain in the middle of the floor from which rose noxious odors. Now and then gray rats ventured from crevices to slither obscenely along the wall and disappear again. Lance's cot was no more than a block of stones built out from the wall, with a crude straw mattress and one thin, filthy blanket. Water dripped somewhere with a monotonous echo.

Lance hunched on the cot, blanket shawled about his resolute shoulders. He might have imagined a more comfortable incarceration, but this grim cell seemed more fitting. This was the true martyr's lot; this was how they imprisoned Robert Ryan when he played John the Baptist. Lance just wished he could have gotten Letti into bed before they took him away.

He had never cheated on Letti. Only the Lord knew how often he'd been tempted, considering her baffling aversion to sex. Maybe God would give him a sympathetic discount on his secret fantasies, since they remained in the realm of dream. The very gates of hell could not prevail against a virtuous man.

Time passed. Lance shivered in his blanket, jerking in revulsion when a transient rat nuzzled at his leg. John the Baptist did not have to put up with rats. Lance fastidiously deleted rodents from his picturesque suffering but left the water-drip for atmosphere.

The bolt withdrew from the door with a hollow clang; the portal groaned open on rusty hinges. A smallish man in a dun monk's robe entered, nodding pleasantly to Lance.

"I am Wyclif, sir. To look after you. How are you getting on?"

Lance regarded him out of a sea of suffering. "Are you a Christian?"

"I am, sir. They presumed you would want one. But this place . . ." Wyclif took in the verminous cell. "Excessively of my era. You might at least have imagined the Tower."

"Are you born again?"

"Once was enough in my time." Wyclif's smile was gentle but wry. "I translated the first English Bible. To Rome, that was a suffing Protestantism."

Lance's historical perspective was landlocked by Technicolor movies. "The King James Bible?"

"Oh, goodfellow, centuries before that. Edward and the Church barely forgave me. But there is news: be of good cheer. Even now, well in advance of trial, puissant counsel flies to your defense. One Peter Helm by name."

Puissant sounded suspiciously foreign to Lance.

"Strong," the mild little cleric clarified. "Formidable: an excellent term for Master Helm. Not warm, not a merry man, sooth, but impressive. He will come anon."

Lance was not very reassured. "The Devil will find someone just as strong for his side."

Not yet, Wyclif warranted. Many had volunteered for defense before Master Helm was chosen, whereas not one tatter-gowned haunter of shire courts could be found to prosecute. "Meanwhile there has come a visitor for you. A woman."

Lance brightened. He got up quickly, hoping. "My wife?"

Wyclif looked dubious. "If your wife wears trews like unto the skin of a leopard and hair of a shade to beggar description, well she may be." He withdrew, leaving the door open. "I will admit her."

He did. Lance stared open-mouthed at his visitor. The electric pink hair riveted him; he *had* seen her before and not long ago. *Revelations* was more forgettable.

"Hey, Lance," she confided breathily. "Activism turns me on."

The prisoner was an innocent. "Are you a tempter?"

"Me? No way." She peeked carefully around the cell door. "Unless you want some good shit."

"Uh . . . ?"

"Grass. Great stuff, no stems or seeds."

"No, thank you. I don't smoke."

"Hey, neither do I. Cigarettes are carcinogenic."

"Uh—who are you?"

"Scheherazade Ginsberg—this month anyway. My horoscope and biorhythms always tell me when to change. You're the most relevant activist I've met since the Weathermen. Kee-fucking-*rist.*" The T-shirted wraith hugged her thin frame, shivering. "It's cold in here. Can I sit down?"

Scheherazade curled up on the cot, sneakered feet tucked under her. Her manner was intense and darting, like a streetwise squirrel or some small nocturnal forager ready to jump at sudden danger, but otherwise intent on the business of survival. She jittered with the cold. Lance draped his blanket around her bony shoulders; she appreciated the courtesy more than the malodorous blanket.

"Hey, man—can I call you Lance?—why do you have to stay in this dump? I've hit some crummy crash pads, but this is the definite pits."

"This is the mirror of my spirit," Lance muttered hollowly. "The way I feel."

"It's a downer. This is the tenth floor of the Hilton Hereafter, full of Christians and saints and people like that," she protested with an unbelieving survey of the walls, "but the other pads got it all over this."

"A martyr's suffering is internal."

"Oh, that is so true, Lance. Your principles really turn me on. What's your sign? What day were you born?"

"November ninth."

"I knew it!" she yipped. "Scorpio! Me too. Scorpio men are the sexual most. Especially now when I'm into my hetero phase. What a *rush.* You don't mind if I feel a little horny along with respecting your principles?"

Long sojourner in a sexual wasteland, Lance didn't mind at all, though her language brought an involuntary blush. Scheherazade's moot charms trebled with the added spice of availability, but . . . there were proprieties. "Look, Miss—"

"Ginsberg. And it's Ms. Miss is sexist."

"What I wanted to say, I'm married."

Scheherazade was unfazed. "Honor is a trip in men of our sign."

"Sign." With a dawning sense of sexual rescue came recollection. "You were there when they took me in. You hit somebody with a sign."

The pink hair bobbed in vigorous affirmation. "I'm an activist."

"They arrested you too."

"Nah, that kind of bust is Kleenex. I got a great lawyer used to be with ACLU. He got scragged by the Klan in '68, same time as me."

In all his limited experience with women, Lance had never confronted anyone like her; certainly not in Neosho Falls. "The Klan killed you?"

"No, just I died that same year. Which was a very heavy year for protest, lemme tell you." And she did. She held vigils, got blisters and then calluses carrying signs, busted three times for possession and once for obstructing a public sidewalk, but these were only prelude to greatness. When a nuclear reactor was built and the tapering towers almost finished, Scheherazade was called to glory.

"You gotta see it." She bounded off the cot, blanket flapping around her. "I mean if you want to be significant, if you want to count, you gotta *do* something, right?"

"Right," said Lance, losing himself in her charisma.

"Like you did for the President. I climbed up on that scaffolding at four in the morning, like in the real dark night of the soul, and was it ever. Splinters, you wouldn't believe. And when the sun came up, and those mothers came to finish the reactor, there I was—"

Her glory built with symphonic excitement. Lance couldn't tear his eyes from her.

"—with TEN COTTONPICKING STICKS OF TNT WRAPPED AROUND ME!"

"Ohmigod! Where'd you get—?"

"Guerrillas network." She slighted the question with professional cool. "We get. You need an Uzi? Anyway, there I am, ready to sacrifice myself for a safe America."

"Scheherazade—"

"Call me Sherry."

"What you were doing, that's against the law."

"Not the people's law, man. There I am in a dynamite bra, giving the finger to the pigs down below who can't get to me because I sawed off the scaffold, and they're bullhorning up at me: COME DOWN AT ONCE. LEAVE THE DEVICE ON THE STEPS AND COME DOWN! And me, I didn't say a word, just—"

Her thin arms opened beyond the cell to the unlimited vistas of freedom. The blanket fell from her nobby frame like frail mortality surrendering the spirit of Joan at Rouen. "Just opened my arms and let the leaflets float on the wind. Beautiful meaningful poems of peace and protest, snowflakes of significance falling and falling on the shit of corruption. Man—terminal joy."

Lance had to rise, had to go to her with the blanket to cover again her brave shoulders. "You died for what you believed in. You died for a cause."

"No." Scheherazade confessed in the small voice of a disappointed mouse. "A downer. Like making it all night and not being able to come."

As stated, Lance was a blusher. "Well . . . what happened?"

"I forgot the matches. Not one fucking light. Lance, can you relate to how I *felt?*"

Lance searched for some consolation. "I always say it's the thought that counts."

The pigs hassled her for that, she explained, but she looked fabulous on TV for a couple of days and even greater when her lawyer got her out on a technicality and she went back to New York to link up with the Weathermen.

"The who?"

Scheherazade couldn't believe he didn't know. "You are so historically deprived. You don't remember the Weathermen in 1968?"

"I was eight," he defended himself. "I didn't even go to the movies by myself in 1968."

The Weathermen, Scheherazade informed him in institutional tones, were *the* activists of that turbulent time. "But they needed a good hand with explosives because now and then they blew themselves up."

Lance was aghast. "Oh, Sherry. Is that—? You didn't deserve to die like that."

"I didn't," she denied with a note of annoyance. "It isn't relevant how I died."

Lance found her hand and held on tight. "It is to me. You were a friend to come and see me. Will you tell a friend?"

"Well . . . I never told a single soul about this. I got this pad in the East Village. Not much better than this place. You really oughta think something better like soon—and next day I'm to meet with a Weather connection on First Avenue. A real fox, I heard, and I was just in the right phase for her, so I decided to dye my hair symbolically." She lowered her eyes in embarrassment. "This is a real bummer. Promise me you won't laugh."

"I wouldn't. I swear."

"So I'm in the bathtub with the radio on the edge, just a little spaced, grooving on the Stones. And the radio fell in the water."

The implication sank in; Lance winced. "You mean—"

"My biorhythms are very sensitive to electricity."

A heavy iron key turned in the rusty lock. Wyclif peered around the door. "Time, good lady. Master Candor's counsel will be here soon."

"No, please," Lance protested. "She's the only visitor I've had."

"Alas. A few minutes more then." Wyclif obligingly withdrew.

Scheherazade mewed in sympathy. "You mean your own wife hasn't been to see you?"

"She's been very busy with my appeals and . . . and things like that." Though Lance knew with some bitterness that these efforts would be mostly spent at Letti's makeup table. She would not look tacky making an appeal. Quickly Scheherazade moved close to comfort the forlorn prisoner.

"Don't lose hope, baby. Being a hero is fraught with danger. You blow up a god, you have to expect a few bad vibes."

"Hope. I did what I had to. But why is it all so lonely?"

"You're not alone," Scheherazade urged. "You're meaningful."

But what if his case was lost, what of the disgrace? Not one of his ancestors had ever been Below Stairs, not even to visit. Letti wouldn't feel right going there to see him even for a day. The Candors were respected among the Blessed Elect of Kansas, except for one great-uncle who strayed and became a Christian Scientist. "I stood for my principles as much as any Christian, but no one's come to see me. Just you."

"Baby, baby," Scheherazade crooned into his cheek. "You're not alone. You've got me now. You'll never walk alone."

Lance knuckled at his moist eyes and tried to smile bravely. "You're a real person."

"I always turn to the classics for comfort."

"Like the Bible."

"And Shakespeare and music; heavy stuff like that. Listen."

As she began to recite, the mellow sound of a harp and soft strings warmed the gloom of Lance's cell, and then sweet feminine voices. The melody and words were indeed a recognized classic.

"As you walk through a storm, hold your head up high, and don't be afraid of the dark."

"Yes," he whispered, inspired in the very depths of despair. "So deep, so true."

"At the end of the storm is a golden sky and the sweet silver song of a lark."

Lance's heart swelled with the music and reborn strength. "I'm so glad you know Shakespeare."

"Walk on through the wind—"

"Yes, Sherry. Yes, I will!"

"Walk on through the rain—"

The orchestra billowed in a forte under her recitation and with it the chorus of clear young girls' voices. Lance felt apotheosis had not after all been denied him.

"—though your dreams be tossed and blown. Walk on, walk on, with hope in your heart—"

"And you'll never walk alone." Lance's hope soared with the dulcet chorus. "You'll *never* walk alone."

"The wisdom of the ages, Lance."

"Oh, Sherry." He hugged her close to him, ratty blanket and all. "Letti would never understand anything so deep or tender or real."

They clung together in a sweet miasma of strings and French horns. Lance's eyes closed tight to shut out the trial and Letti, all but the moment and this truth in his arms as the gorgeous music faded.

"Sherry?"

"Mm?"

"What's a hetero phase?"

"Never mind, Lance," she whispered, content. "It's now."

6

Light Speed

Scheherazade had seriously argued with Lance to redecorate his idea of a cell before she came again because even the Jesus freaks next floor up had swinging pads. Nevertheless he clung out of principle to the medieval ambience, modifying only the excessive damp.

Wyclif said his lawyer would come anon, which Lance learned meant later on. He was glad he'd eased up on the damp. As promised, Peter Helm came anon, bringing his own cold with him. He did not offer his hand. Lance felt the man avoided human contact. He sensed an intimidating power of will in Helm's small frame, like a V-8 engine in a Volkswagen. A more precise observer would note that the ascetic cast of features did not quite go with the modern gray suit and vest. Helm's was not a face or expression one found in this century. He glanced in passing at his client before surveying the stone cell with open disapproval.

"Forget this. Distracting and unnecessary."

With no deference to the prisoner, Helm altered the space to half-timbered plaster walls with an open mullioned window. A dark wood table appeared with two severe chairs. The result was tidier, but Lance had often felt the same coldness and apprehension in a dentist's waiting room.

"Sit down, Candor."

"I guess you're my lawyer. Did Letti pick you out?"

Helm paused in donning a pair of steel-rimmed spectacles austere as the rest of him. "Who is Letti?"

"My wife."

"Indeed? No," said Helm in a tone tinged with reproof. "I was retained by those with your best interests at heart. I requested this case—which we will now consider and win for the greater glory of God." Spoken not for encouragement but as fact cold and objective as the delicate little barrister himself. "That woman who came, that was your wife?"

"No, she's a friend. A revolutionary, she said."

"Let her revolve elsewhere," Helm decreed. "You will not admit her again."

As with his every utterance, Helm's instructions did not invite argument. For all that, Scheherazade had touched and left Lance with some reckless germ of defiance. He didn't even apologize to God for the uncharacteristic profanity. *The hell I won't. Just who are you anyway . . . ?*

A good question. The man currently known as Peter Helm believed in the Elect of God more deeply than his client could ever hope to. Better educated even in his own century, the liberation from Rome only unleashed the northern darkness of his soul. Without the buffer of an orthodox clergy, God impacted on Helm's passionate soul like a heavy stone in soft clay. The direct spiritual descendant of the Manicheans, he saw God as iron, the world filth, men weak vessels and their evil part and parcel with the good. The damned were legion, the Elect few and already numbered. Only an absolute theocracy was acceptable to the God of Peter Helm; only absolutes in every smallest moment of life, awake or asleep, were safeguards for men.

Lance might have seen that thin scholar's face in any comprehensive encyclopedia. The surviving likeness in pen and ink catches him with eyes downcast to one side as if communing with some tender poetic thought. The Protestant equivalent of the Inquisition, the first to commandeer the right to search into the undusted corners of private lives, proclaiming no man free from God's scrutiny as it flamed in those ironically sensitive eyes. The irony was deeper than Lance would ever grasp. No sower ever planted a bitterer or more tenacious seed in Europe or early America—but then even Nazis thought their causes noble. Another bookish little pedant, Heinrich Himmler, said during a visit to a concentration camp: "To be able to kill like this and remain decent, undeterred from the pure end . . ."

None would have understood or agreed so quickly as the man called Helm.

The vast emptiness of the Void crushed the frail individuality of post-life humans. They crossed it only out of necessity. Few paused to admire the view. Only two men remained there by choice, though from dichotomous motives. Peter Helm and Joshua Speed.

When Peter Helm tore loose from mortality, he expected no less than the City of God to which he had devoted the faith and efforts of a stringent lifetime. He found only Topside and Barion, mundane as the existence left behind. He remained just long enough to obliterate his name from Barion's records. Helm was shaken. Where was the ordered cosmos in which he had invested his life? He had expected outer darkness as well as the Citadel of Faith. He found only Below Stairs, entered by stealth and left abruptly. In the hell of his rock-ribbed faith, Helm had expected to find Martin Luther and a full complement of Romish popes roasting together in eternal flame. He found a nebulous state more garish than Topside but as ordinary, with suffering only for those who briefly insisted on it, and an enormous amount of raucous enjoyment.

Helm refused to believe in the reality of either establishment. They were devilish illusions, final tests of the spirit devised by God without Whom not even Satan could lift a finger. Helm departed again across the Void—rapidly at first, then more slowly as his mind cleared of confusion. The Void terrified him, so he must battle with his own fear. Like a desert, the emptiness could kill men unfit for it. He challenged the Void. Nothingness pressed in on him until his spirit felt constricted and crushed small as a pebble, or threatened to pluck him apart piece by piece. Helm fought both.

He despised his fear, observing contemptuously from cold detachment how the timorous human spirit quailed in this waste place of contrasting light and shadow. The beauty of creation, the slow turning of Earth and Moon within the larger wheel of stars meant nothing to Peter Helm. God and His City were somewhere and Hell very real.

These illusions were part of the test of his will. He hated them. All his life he had expounded absolutes and certitudes. Only when he had mastered his fear of this non-place did he return secretly to Topside to forge new identity and wait his time.

The name "Helm" came easily, that which directed the course of a ship. He had steered unerringly for his people in Switzerland until his death. With a new name and blank slate, Peter Helm waited out the centuries to come again. Trained in law, steel-tempered to inflexible principles, the post-life exile forced him to recognize the cyclical nature of human history. Out of his own time came the dissolution of the old order and the formation of the new. Fickle Man threw off faith and played with his mind, created an age of secular reason, turned from the steadfast contemplation of God and rationalized a best of all possible worlds. In the cold Void, Helm laughed and waited. America came, the very hard-eyed true believers he'd known in life. They struggled, survived, grew powerful, eventually flaccid and easily led. Only Helm's faithful, the vindictive poor, did not change. With technology grew their feeling of personal impotence and need once more for simple absolutes. When certain very recognizable men took the bitch goddess Media and used it to reach those forgotten multitudes with the old hellfire truths of existence, Helm knew his time was near. When the Devil spewed his secular lies over Topside and the inane Candor hurled rejection with his bomb, Helm knew that time had come.

Lance Candor was not important, merely pathetic and self-involved. Such men were not steel for the Sword of God. Steel did not hunger or need but entered the flesh and subdued it. However, like the inert object that trips up great cause and makes it stumble forward, Candor was a very usable catalyst.

HELM TO DEFEND CANDOR
TOPSIDE SPLIT OVER HIT
VOCAL MAJORITY: WE LOVE LANCE!
FUNDYS SEE TRIAL HOTTEST SINCE FALL OF
SATAN

Peter Helm made several appearances on TSTV as the trial date neared. Coyul was impressed. For the usual run of Reconstructionist—if he was one—Helm came off with a first-rate media image, clean-cut and photogenic, a cinch for a Senate win in a conservative Earthside state. Definitely an A-list personality, as the yuppies would say.

"That man could sell sand to Arabs."

"Utterly in control," Purji agreed, wondering how such an icon could be at once charismatic and repellant. "Perhaps because we're not human."

"He's like a dancing cobra, graceful and terribly efficient. Who am I going to put up against him?" Coyul despaired. "Right now it's Christians ten, Lions zip."

For prudent reasons: no one wanted to take a case already tried and lost in the popular mind and press. Socrates said so yesterday, Blackstone the day before that. Darrow wouldn't touch it, firmly retired to rocking chairs and fly-tying. He was Coyul's last, best hope.

"Clarence, for old times' sake take the case. Helm doesn't give a litigational hoot in hell about Candor; it's me he wants."

The Great Defender snorted. "No kidding?" He selected a Panetela and offered the box to Coyul. "He wants a lot more than you, Prince. This case is tapped into the sixty-four-million-dollar question. Man: is he to live by truth or a sugar-coated fairy tale? Bright heaven, dark hell, once a year at Christmas a nod to magis, mangers and mercy. Truth has never been a hot item even with free dishes. Sure you won't have a cigar?"

"I don't need a cigar. I need help!"

"Uh-huh." For long hedonistic moments, Darrow savored the fine white ash growing on his Panetela, recalling Coyul's help to his own cause during a few historic days in Tennessee. He owed one to the Prince, at least a dollop of sound advice. "Not me, Coyul, I'm too well known. I'd kill any chance you have with the Candor fans. But you do need an American. I mean a down-home boy who doesn't look or sound city-fied."

Good counsel. At its rural heart, America had always been anti-intellectual. No Fundamentalist, from Billy Sunday to Jimmy Swaggart, ever exhorted his flock to repentance or even remittance with a Harvard accent. Down-home or not, Helm already had the Far Right in his pocket.

"Speed." Darrow puffed at his cigar and blew three perfect smoke rings. "Joshua Speed is your man."

Coyul's memory for names was fairly reliable back to Ur of the

Chaldees, but he came up empty on this one. "Must be age. An absolute blank."

"That needn't be his real name. For that matter, how real is Peter Helm? Might be enlightening to check records on both."

"Stop being a lawyer. If you know who Speed is—"

"Didn't say that."

"Or where he is—"

"I don't." The Great Defender vouchsafed a lawyer's smile that said much without compromising one iota. "If I once made a wild guess about someone I'd respect under any name, I'd assume he had his reasons for secrecy and treat the matter as privileged."

Clarence Darrow gave his whole attention to the best of all possible cigars.

COYUL FROM FELIM, RECORDS RETRIEVAL: ALL PRAISE TO ALLAH, THE ONE TRUE GOD—

GET ON WITH IT, FELIM. THIS IS URGENT.

REUR INQUIRY JOSHUA SPEED AKA TEN ADDITIONAL ALIASES. REAL NAME DELETED BY REQUEST.

MARVELOUS, FELIM. DATE OF BIRTH, DEATH?

DELETED AS ABOVE.

WHO AUTHORIZED DELETION? DON'T YOU HAVE ANY SECURITY AROUND HERE?

AUTHORITY BARION.

Why would Barion do that? Coyul could find no satisfactory answer.

TRANSMIT ALL AVAILABLE DATA.

FIRST ENTRY: TOPSIDE 1910 (INFIDEL CALENDAR) KNOWN AS SPEED, DEFENDED SAMUEL CLEMENS AKA MARK TWAIN AGAINST PROTESTANT COALITION, CHARGE OF SEDITIOUS ATHEISM. ACQUITTAL. VARIOUS SUBSEQUENT CASES TOPSIDE, BELOW STAIRS. MORE TO FOLLOW . . .

Coyul gleaned as much as he could from the meager data. Joshua Speed: trial lawyer, some experience probate, constitutional law. At least one murder case, defense, client acquitted. Predeceased his wife, never rejoined her in post life.

COYUL TO FELIM: WIFE'S NAME?

NO DATA. FILE ENDS WITH PERSONAL NOTE BY BARION.

Curiouser and curiouser. Barion had circumvented procedure only once before, to Coyul's knowledge, in leaving all file references to

Yeshua of Nazareth in skeletal Aramaic notes. As in Speed's case, at subject request. There was little enough to go on.

TRANSMIT BARION NOTE.

"Speed is an unusual case," Barion wrote. "Physically his abnormalities combined with his perceived motives to make him an object of ridicule in his time. Classic ectomorph, acromegalic condition, face and hands. Manic depressive, tending toward suicide though not severely. Periods of brilliance alternating with melancholy and enervating guilt. Self-taught, self-motivated or -obstructed, depending on humor. Reputation contradictory and all deserved. I found greatness, generosity, patience, moral courage mixed with naked calculation and—not coldness, not as the word is generally construed, but a tendency to distance himself from others while remaining fixed on objectives. One of the least loved and clearest thinking men of his time. For post life he asked only silence and solitude. I gave him both."

Once again the Great Defender was of some help. He just might suggest where to look for the elusive Speed. "Just a wild guess."

"Clarence, my sands run down. Dispatch."

Darrow remained circumspect: there was a certain lady, imperious, social, nutty as a California salad, who had expected on death to find her husband Topside but never did. A society woman who considered Topside a barely acceptable address and wouldn't be caught dead Below Stairs—and yet the lady had departed abruptly for that environ about the time Coyul arrived Topside.

"Looking for Speed, you think?"

"What do you think?"

"You could have *told* me, Clarence."

"I just did. Might be a dead end, probably is. On the other hand . . ."

"God." Coyul just then wished for such metaphoric extremities as heavens he could appeal to. "And they call *me* King of Lawyers."

"Only fair," Darrow allowed. "Called me the Devil in Tennessee."

"They called you worse in Chicago." Coyul was already out the door. "And they were right!"

COYUL, TOPSIDE TO JUDAS, BELOW STAIRS: JAKE, MOST URGENT. PLEASE LOCATE JOSHUA SPEED. ADVISE REAL NAME IF KNOWN. WHO

IS HE, WHERE IS HE? DOES YESHUA KNOW? REPEAT: MOST URGENT
AND MOST CONFIDENTIAL.

When he died, a redundant violence at the end of a larger one, the
man later called Joshua Speed arrived Topside in the company of astonished atheists, intrigued intellectuals and hymn-singing hordes of the
faithful looking for vindication or at least definition. The untidy *laissez-
faire* administration of Barion hardly distressed Speed, who was used to
it, but the small improvement over life was a letdown. He did not
remain Topside for long. Below Stairs, rowdy and eclectic, offered no
more permanent inducement. Sick to his soul of a steady stream of
people all wanting something of him—profit, advantage or naked re-
venge—Speed longed for solitude. Above all he desired distance from
his troublesome, abrasive wife. He realized he was as difficult, a morose,
unreachable man coupled with a woman needing more affection than he
ever kept in stock for individuals.

Shucked of life, then, he pondered where to go.

"There is the music of the spheres," a poet suggested.

"There is the wind that blows between the worlds," advised another
artist, straining metaphor as usual.

"There's the Void," said an ashcan realist. "Get lost in it. You ain't
missing a thing."

Never lost, not the singular mind of Joshua Speed with its intense
light and sudden, deep shadows. In the Void he sought a self cleansed of
the soot of a lifetime, eyes unfilmed at last and able to see infinity. More
than all these, a self freed of name and legend.

The Void suited him. He floated for decades in spiritual free-fall as
the Moon circled Earth, Earth wheeled about the Sun, and the Sun
roared and rolled through its own revolution in an even greater wheel.
Passing beyond the red storms of Jupiter, at last even the blessed silence
of space palled on Speed, became unaccountably oppressive. He felt
weaker and weaker as the world that had borne him dwindled to a tiny
point of pale blue light. Perhaps there were limits even here to freedom
and going on would dissipate him further until nothing remained. He
didn't miss life, but neither did he want to disappear.

"A healthy consideration, Mr. Speed. Need a hand?"

After the silent years, the gentle voice startled Josh Speed. He looked
over his left shoulder to see Barion ranging along his port side. "There

are limits even for me," Barion admitted. "Feeling bored or are you game for more?"

"If I can find some meaning." Speed felt himself reviving rapidly. "Are you feeding me energy?"

"Just a booster. You read a bit weak. We're a long way out."

"Take me as far as I can go."

"Curious?"

"Call it that. I want to know whether knowing all this will frighten me."

Barion laughed. "A healthy ego as well. Human to the core: how does all this relate to the reality of you? Come on, then. As far as we can, we'll weigh your soul against infinity."

They shot outward together into deeper space at unimaginable velocity. The solar system became a mere blur of light, pulled together in the distance as they plunged deeper into black space where whole galaxies were no more than distant jewel-work on stygian velvet, yet Speed felt no terror or disappointment.

"All of this exists for itself," he murmured. "No part of me."

Barion's glance was not quite inscrutable just then; one could discern admiration. "Yes."

"But *I* exist." Speed exulted in his own kind of victory. "A terrible, fearsome beauty that doesn't have to be about me, though I'm still here. We understand as we can, I guess."

"I had to learn patience too," Barion admitted. "It was that or chuck in the towel."

"Where are we going, Barion? Us. Humans: where's the end for us?"

"There is no end, Josh. Where do you want to go, and how much excess baggage are you ready to leave behind?"

Speed couldn't accept that all at once, human enough to need an end, a closure. He shot suddenly light-years beyond his companion—"Josh, don't! We're too far out!"

—then, as if he'd stumbled on a solid obstruction, Speed cartwheeled out of control, end over end. He was barely conscious when Barion caught up with him.

"Enough?"

Speed shook his head to clear it, groggy and croaking. "I just . . . like to get at the heart of things."

"You're a rare breed," Barion told him as they streaked Earthward across ebony and fire. "Not many have dared this. Yeshua, Einstein, a fellow called Helm. A few others tried but gave it up. Too lonely for most. No drama. Not about them. Want a job, Josh?"

No, thanks just the same. Speed preferred the Void.

"Pity. Interesting case," Barion tempted. "Might keep your hand in. There's a Missouri man named Sam Clemens who badly needs a lawyer just now."

"Mark Twain. I met him Below Stairs." For the moment, the deeply etched downturn of Speed's mouth was not quite so sad. "Sentimental, not too deep, but still . . ." He broke off the thought, but Barion read it anyway.

Yes, those he loved, he loved fiercely. You envy that. "Funny as ever," Barion noted casually, "and already in trouble."

"Who with?"

"American Fundamentalists, who else?" After five million years, Barion might have predicted Twain's difficulties with such intransigent folk. The Fundamentalists considered themselves the salt of the earth and quick as the next fellow to laugh at a joke, but saw nothing funny in *Captain Stormfield, Letters from the Earth* or Twain's latest satire on the respected Reverend Strutley, a pillar of Topside.

"What do they charge?"

"Libel, slander, all with the prefix 'atheistic' for public consumption. The Plaintiff, Reverend Strutley, has spared no rhetoric."

"Strutley." Speed rummaged memory and found something. "Chataugua tent preacher a few years back."

"That's the one."

Speed's expression underwent a subtle change from melancholy to something less pleasant. "Never used to let up on—what was it?—the modesty of sacred womanhood in dress and deportment."

"Did you read Twain's *1601?*"

"I have." Speed chuckled. "Funny but awful raw."

"Well, it's nothing compared to the new stuff. He needs a good lawyer, Josh."

Speed shrugged. "What the hell. Why not?"

Good—though first Barion suggested a radical change of image: shave, new hairstyle, a whole new concept of wardrobe. People perceived surfaces; Josh Speed's was something of an institution.

By this name or that, appearance altered, Speed tried an occasional case Topside, always returning afterward to the Void. He found it pure and clean and enough of a mystery to be endlessly fascinating. He was a man who took his reality neat.

JUDAS, BELOW STAIRS TO COYUL, TOPSIDE: SORRY, KNOW JOSHUA SPEED BY THAT NAME ALONE. LOCATED HIM BY LUCK BEFORE HE WANDERED OFF AGAIN INTO THE COSMIC OUTBACK. ACCEPTS CASE, WANTS MEETING TOPSIDE, ALL PARTICULARS RE CANDOR. BSTV NEWS TEAM ALSO ENROUTE TO COVER TRIAL. WISH YOU WERE HERE: WILKSEY BOOTH A SMASH AS ME IN PASSION PLAY. HAVEN'T LOOKED SO GOOD SINCE MY BAR MITZVAH. YESHUA SENDS BEST, LOVE FROM ALL—XXX—JAKE.

Joshua Speed shambled into Coyul's salon, ducking his head to clear the doorframe. Six foot three or more, he looked as if he'd come to that excessive measure through a careless mistake in assembly. None of his outsized parts seemed quite to match, from the huge, gnarled hands to the curiously overpronounced cheekbones. The short salt-and-pepper hair only accented the abnormal exaggeration of the features. The rumpled trousers and corduroy jacket with leather-patched elbows might have been slept in. Speed reminded Coyul of a sad horse.

And vaguely of someone else. Coyul experienced a rush of *déjà vu*.

Somewhere in his passionate need to be forgotten, Speed had learned to mask his mind, though Coyul perceived chinks here and there. He read in the man a vast sorrow and personal loss. Not much sentiment but, now and then, quite clear in the eyes, a melancholy beauty.

Where have I seen you before?

"Speed, sir."

"Delighted, Mr. Speed; please sit down." Coyul extended a cordial hand, irritated that he couldn't place the man at all. Speed settled his length by ungainly sections in as much of the inadequate chair as would contain him. He donned a pair of rimless spectacles and produced a sheaf of notes.

"I see by the television that Defense is very confident. I'll ask for a continuance; we don't have much time in any case."

The voice, high and thin but unmistakably American, was the most maddeningly familiar thing about the man. "I want to thank you for taking a case even Darrow wouldn't touch."

"Clarence is no fool," said Speed in a soft drawl that could harden suddenly into a steel weapon. "They're after your hide; Candor's only a flag."

"Do you know the defense counsel Peter Helm?"

Speed didn't, not personally. "Seen him on the television, that's all. Shaping this case into a tent revival, so-o, let's trim his lamp." The steel trap shut. "Drop the criminal charge and make it a civil case with yourself as plaintiff."

Not being a lawyer, Coyul didn't follow immediately. "Where's the advantage?"

"Taking Helm's away. I may look like the south end of a northbound mule, but I'd never try an emotional case on the opposition's home ground."

Since the real issue was not Candor—Speed explained—but Coyul's disputed presence, to say nothing of his identity, the case resolved to whoever got his viewpoint across to the jury. In a criminal case prosecution would be constrained to try the act of assault for guilt or innocence. Defense could successfully object to any testimony not directly concerned with that assault, while any doctrinaire hoopla Candor sang on the stand would be admissible.

"But in a *civil* case—invasion of privacy, personal distress, what have you—your own cause can be heard. Mistaken identity, the damage as direct result. Helm will have the hell of a time objecting to that. We don't play his game; he plays ours."

Coyul found himself impressed. "Very good, Josh. Immaculate."

"Obviously you're not the Devil."

"To my occasional regret. Life would be downhill and shady."

"I wouldn't think the pay worth the pain," Speed opined. "Who's on the bench?"

"Marcus Aurelius."

"Yes." Speed seemed pleased with the choice. "Literate, reflective . . ."

"And tolerant for his time. Dear old Gibbon suggested him."

"Your friend Purji who admitted me?" Speed poised a pencil over his notes. "She's of your own race?"

"Yes. Like mine, her human form is a convenience—most of the time. She tends to overdo."

"I forgive her," was Speed's laconic gallantry. "Spent some time as an object of worship? A . . . fertility goddess?"

"Purji does nothing by halves."

"We can use an experienced deity on our side. Expert witness." Speed block-printed PURJI and drew a box around the name. Then another box which he left blank. "And one ace in the hole."

"Ace?"

"Just a cud I want to chew before making up my mind. Surprise witnesses are always effective." Speed wadded his notes into a baggy side pocket. "You agree to a civil case?"

"I'm in your hands." Literally. Coyul's offered hand was engulfed in Speed's mammoth paw—as Purji's mind whispered into his—

Darling? Mr. Helm is here. Please take him off my hands.

Trouble?

I know it's silly of me, but he's so like a Keljian reformer who once ran me through with a spear before I could discorporate. Sorry to get emotional.

I would too, dear. Send him in. "Enter the villain," Coyul stage-whispered to his counsel. "Here's your chance to size up Peter Helm."

When Peter Helm entered, Coyul was privately amused by the contrast between the two barristers. Next to the severely tailored Helm, light and tight in his movements, totally balanced and assured, Speed's most controlled gesture looked like something dislodged and about to fall. Speed rose courteously; introducing them, Coyul thought he saw a flicker of recognition pass between the two men, not so much of person but kind, rival predators on a disputed hunting ground.

"We are prepared," Helm clipped. "I am not altogether happy with the bench. A Christian would be preferable."

"Oh, there were no end of popes keen for the job," Coyul told him. "Lutherans, even a few Unitarians. Aurelius is totally impartial."

"I see." Helm allowed himself a small, frigid smile. "Let it stand. Ready, Mr. Speed?"

"Well, like a fresh egg in a cold hen house, I could use a few more days in the shell. My client is dropping the criminal charge for a civil plaint."

Coyul read an instant of consternation in Peter Helm, but no more. That mind was masked as efficiently as Speed's. "Very astute, sir. I will request a brief continuance to adjust."

"There is a vague popular belief that lawyers are necessarily dishonest." Speed grinned ruefully. "Let's discourage that, Mr. Helm. I daresay we've both seen base instincts in the employ of noble causes. Fair fight?"

"A just one, Mr. Speed."

They shook hands. Like prizefighters, Coyul thought. "And I will release the long-suffering Candor," he said, seeing them both to the door. "Old Wyclif won't be sorry; the damp's been cruel to his arthritis. See you in court, gentleman."

"Join me in a drink?" Speed invited Helm.

"I never drink, sir."

"What a pity. How's your poker?"

"Nor do I gamble."

"You're gambling now," Speed reminded him. "Just wanted to see how you bet."

7

Them old live forever, die tomorrow blues

CANDOR TO BE RELEASED
CIVIL TRIAL SEEN AS SURPRISE MOVE
HELM ON TRIAL: "NO COMMENT"

"How deceptive appearance can be. I will not underestimate Mr. Speed."

Helm stopped pacing and halted, hands on narrow hips, glaring at his aide, the Senator from Wisconsin. "That bucolic countryman of yours has neatly removed our whole initiative."

The Senator had a moon face, thinning hair and a disconcerting tendency to giggle at inappropriate moments; at other times he looked merely ponderous or paranoid. Working for Helm was old times returned for the Senator, possibly old power restored. Conspiracy had always inspired him. "You want me to stay on Speed?"

"Anything you can find. We need a lever. There is a new word in your country, something to do with . . . Watergate? Those who obtained information quietly."

"Plumbers." The Senator giggled. "I've got a dozen or more here and Below Stairs."

"Employ them," Helm directed. "No man blanks his record or changes his name to no purpose. Find out who Joshua Speed really is."

"Come to think of it," the Senator said, "I don't even know who you are."

"Trust me, Joseph. We stand for the same principle. Speed wears the black hat and I the white. Loose your plumbers."

"Love of my endless life." Purji stroked the back of Coyul's neck as he chorded moodily at the piano. "When this ridiculous trial is done, can we talk about us?"

"Immortal longings?"

"Oh . . . twinges of permanence." Purji doodled on the treble keys. "Time we grew up." Plink! "Settled down." Plunk!

"What do you call this, a coffee break?"

"I'm talking union," Purji yearned plaintively. "Permanence. Children. Possibilities."

Coyul listened sympathetically though distracted. Peter Helm bothered him as Cassius once distressed Caesar: he couldn't quite corner the problem, but there it was like indigestion. "Such as?"

"Think, for example, what we could give this world in the way of a messiah. Let your mind toy with the notion."

Coyul toyed. The notion was unique, the image unsettling: Purji as madonna, a humble manger, magis, genuflecting livestock and a Miklos Rosza soundtrack. Unlikely. On the other hand, given Purji's tastes, who'd buy a messiah born in the Plaza Hotel?

"Meanwhile," she conspired, "before the trial dampens all of your *esprit,* let's throw a party."

From the social page: Sheila Seeword, "Topside Tattler."
Latest from the Salon: cool as vodka over ice on the eve of the Candor trial (isn't Lance the cutest?), we hear Coyul and his glamorous live-in Purji are planning a bash for a Bronze Age jet set called the Algonquin Round Table. We were *not* invited by the pulchritudinous P. —but girls, let's be honest. Dead or alive, anyone with that little cellulite is not for real. The official press kit line on Purji is that she's an alien like Coyul. The *real* dirt, our spies tell us, is her background in one of those pray-and-play TV ministries where the rectory is the local El Sleazo Motel. Will she sue or just write her memoirs? *Quo vadis, Domine?*

The party was a success from the first vivacious arrivals, the ubiquitous Oscar already at the white piano when Purji, a definition of desire in a velvet gown slit far up fabulous thighs, draped herself over the top. Purji loved scotch but had not yet mastered it. She beamed fuzzily at the dour pianist.

"Cyd Charisse could use your figure. So could I," Oscar noted without missing a beat. "Don't say it, I know. You love me."

"I love indeed," murmured his misty hostess. "I was a goddess of love once."

"How were the hours?"

"Not bad. Holidays were always insane. Very big on benedictions. You smile a lot. 'Always a bridesmaid, never a bride.' " Purji gazed wistfully after her soulmate, who was welcoming Gershwin at the door. "Coyul says you have talent."

"I do. He just came in." Oscar gulped the last of his coffee. "Do you have any Demerol?"

"Oscar!" Lida Simone, Kaufman's current leading lady, slid onto the piano bench, hooking an arm around the pianist's neck. "George just came in. What would it take to make him play one teeny little song for me?"

"George?" Oscar chilled Lida with boreal disgust. "The mere wish at a thousand yards."

"Oh, George!" Lida departed unsteadily on her quest. "Geo-o-rge—"

Across the room, wearing a hunted expression, Kaufman could not shake Ricky Remsleep, late of a sixties rock group, the Assassins—now, through cruel default Kaufman's collaborator on the new musical. Kaufman had naturally wanted Moss Hart; alas, Mossie was pigging out Below Stairs, living high and sleeping until noon, regretting only that everything was free. As for dear Edna—at that moment dispensing iron opinion like sparks from a fire across the Salon—they'd written hits together despite incompatibility. Edna had an Anchorite dedication as a writer. She rose early and, even Topside, walked two miles before downing the first of three solid, sensible meals, and began work just as Kaufman began to think of bed as a place of rest. Currently she was finishing her American Indian novel interrupted by death, a singular inconvenience Edna swore never to repeat—"and *never* call before five, George. You really need to discipline yourself."

And so he was stuck with Ricky Remsleep, whose faint celebrity rested on a mixed-media vaguery for guerrilla theater in 1969, just before he overdosed. Unstoned, Remsleep might do a fresh page or two; more often he clogged the script with grim counterculture significance, tugging now at Kaufman's sleeve, insistent as a hound harrying a preoccupied elk—

"Listen, man, it's gotta be relevant."

"How about a little fun along the way?" Kaufman retorted acidly. "We could sort of sneak it in when your generation wasn't looking, like cyanide in Tylenol. The world did not begin or end with Woodstock. Which reminds me: that guitar the juvenile used to lug around in every scene—"

"Used to?" Ricky bristled, sensing profanation. "He still does. When'd you cut that?"

"Now."

"He's a *rock* singer f'crissake. A revolutionary."

Desperate, Kaufman stepped out of character. He hated physical contact but laid a fatherly hand on Remsleep's shoulder, from which death alone had routed dandruff. "Kid, do you know what revolutionaries grow up to be? Tired businessmen and mothers who might want a laugh at the end of a hard day."

Ricky snarled his contempt and drank, slopping his rum Coke. "Yeah, shit. The ones who lived to fucking sell out the whole movement. You're history, George. You are archaic."

Kaufman cast about for escape—as Lida Simone boozily hooked Remsleep's arm like a brass ring, allowing the harried Kaufman nimble escape from worse-than-death. "Talk to me, Ricky." She nuzzled his ear. "Gershwin is being selfish, moaning about Paulette and 1937, whatever they were, and he won't play 'A Summer Place' for me."

"Neither would I," Ricky declared.

"Oh, I love romantics." Lida aimed an inaccurate kiss at the Remsleep mouth and managed only to dampen his cheek. "Jimmy Webb and Richard Harris . . . will you play your guitar at my wedding?"

"What dude you splicing?"

"My fourth husband again. No, my third. We always had a thing. DOTTIE!" Lida loosed Ricky to pounce on a tiny, horn-rimmed woman and dragoon her close. "Dottie, come talk to me. I love the way you write. Will you come to my wedding?"

Dottie had large, wounded eyes and a tremulous voice. She removed the glasses, gazing at Lida with mournful sincerity. "How could I miss your wedding, dear? The last few were such fun." She readjusted the horn-rims, drifting away. "Excuse me. Mr. Benchley is surrounded by Alec Woollcott and signaling for help."

The piano relinquished under protest by Oscar and Gershwin, a white-jacketed orchestra bumped and slid the dancers through a sinuous tango. In Coyul's expert but absentminded embrace, Purji whirled and dipped with total involvement, head flung back, blond waves flashing—

"Oh, *la.* To be mortal and urgent—darling, do keep your mind on it. I'm dancing with an accomplished coat hanger."

"Sorry." Try as he might to put Peter Helm out of his mind, the man left a too-familiar ring in his ear. An idealist like Speed but with a glacial difference, a seeker of truth without compassion. He reminded Coyul of no one so much as Oliver Cromwell, the same icy zeal that could greatly strive for celestial motives while immolating his best friend, putting ground glass in dog food or even catsup on beef.

The tango ended; Coyul and Purji retrieved their drinks just starboard of a politely drunk Dottie staring through her horn-rims into limbo or perhaps the cozily recalled depths of a certain speakeasy on Fifty-second Street. Coyul took her glass.

"What are you having, love?"

"Not much fun," Dottie slurred.

"I never thought to hear it," Coyul tisked. "Mrs. Parker repeating herself."

"So is the world," she enunciated too carefully. "All they do is remakes. Christ, I hated Hollywood. Purji, you do the most wonderful parties." Dottie dropped her horn-rims into a cavernous handbag and rose precariously. "Even if Lida Simone is cutting me up the back, I will now ask Mr. Benchley to see me home. You mustn't mind Lida," she confided warmly. "We go back forever. I knew her before she was a virgin. Oh, shit! I have to *write* tomorrow," she wailed to Coyul. "God, how I loathe it. I am ghosting one of those 'from the heart of a simple woman' autobiographies. Do you know Letti Candor?"

Regrettably, Coyul did.

Dottie batted her eyes in mime and malice. "Y'all know how lonely li'l her must be without her Lay-ance, living hand-to-mink. Do you

know how much she sounds like my mother-in-law? Good night . . .
Mr. Benchley awaits."

With that seraphic smile and great dignity, Mrs. Parker fell on her
face and remained there. Purji thought to rouse her—but no. "She
seems so peaceful and childlike."

"The Little Match Girl with a blowtorch. Back in a second." Coyul
would spare Benchley the trouble. Where the inert Dottie could no
longer navigate, he transported her instantly home to her own poodle-
strewn bed to slumber without troubled dreams of Metro-Goldwyn-
Mayer.

The party waltzed on, unabated. In one corner, Kaufman whispered
intimately to an appreciative Lida. Oscar was at the piano again, and
Purji waxed sentimental.

"I am *ser*ious, Coyul. I want to settle down. Put in roots. Produce
pernamence. Have children."

Coyul was uncertain about inflicting humans on their offspring. On
the other hand, the world was not ready either.

"But we need purpose," Purji persisted. "With our lifespan we need
more than television or the religious tragedy of Lance Candor. No one
we know goes in for tragedy."

"What then, my love? Shall we seek the central meaning of existence.
Square the circle?"

"Oh, we did all that in school. And look at us. Are we really what
they called us then? Brats, wastrels, dilettantes?"

Coyul abbreviated her lament with a kiss. "You just have the blahs."

"Do not digress. Dottie was right. All our eons are remakes. Stars
explode, worlds die, wars start, lovers part. Myths recycle yet again to
explain the tiresome monkey to himself. I'm so damned tired of it."

"So was I by the rise of Sumer," Coyul admitted. "How about bed.
Our guests can fend for themselves."

"Unhand me, villain! I am feeling *fin de siècle* and very articulate
about it, and you offer mere sleep to knit the raveled sleeve of ennui?"

Coyul's next kiss was more to the point. "I said bed for openers."

Purji softened. "You are a romantic. I am with you, Masked Man,
but not like humans again. Please? Such limited gymnastics. Let's make
love like us for a change. For which"—Purji covered a furtive hiccup—
"bed is super . . . superfluous. Honestly, it's all so sad. Humans. Brief
candles. I think I'm drunk. But I like being drunk, it's the only way I
can manage a good cry without laughing myself to death. Don't you

envy humans, Coyul? I mean, don't you wish sometimes we had just a little of that desperate need for *now?*"

"No," said Coyul as they faded from the party. No one missed them at all.

8

After the ball

Even as Dottie passed out, Lance and Scheherazade enjoyed their own party *à deux* in the Hilton Hereafter. After his release, he might have gone home and even took a faltering step in that direction. But why? he asked himself. Letti had not visited him once, while Sherry came every day, even before he redecorated his room. He wouldn't go home just yet. Letti would learn he had a mind of his own. The moral aspect nagged him at first before Lance sedated his scruples in a triumph of pragmatism. Where women were concerned (and Lance was very) a bird in the Hilton was worth two at home. Scheherazade moved in forthwith, backpack, tantric tapes and all.

Her incendiary influence was reflected in a defiant Ché Guevara poster, militant peace symbols and pink neon LOVE signs sputtering softly here and there about the walls, the whole effect softened to a cerise glow now as they dined by candlelight. Flattering lights and Lance's deprivation set off Ms. Ginsberg at her dramatic best. She was even deeper into her current astrological phase, romantic and intense, hair redone in raven black. To Lance in his need, she was desire itself as she poured the Chianti and set his plate before him with a flourish.

"How can the French think they're gourmets when we were the first with frozen pizza? Hey, this is *très intime.*" Scheherazade touched her glass to his. "Too fucking much."

"Don't curse." But Lance couldn't bring himself to blush or disapprove with his old conviction. Their mood and the ambience adhered to the standards of the very best sherry commercials—a cheery fire on the hearth, romantic shadows, a great many violins, the television muttering white noise in its corner. They'd both grown up with that comforting babble through meals and social gatherings, even lovemaking. Absence would create a vacuum.

Lance let the music take him. "Mantovani. He always does classics."

"It is to die."

"That's how I feel now, Sherry."

"Oh, Lance, me too. I am in sync with all of it. I am one with the universe."

"I just wish—" He hesitated, then tossed his napkin on the table. "It's not right."

She was instantly solicitous. "What, baby?"

"Never mind."

"Don't keep secrets; what are friends for?"

"Why hasn't Letti come? It's been so long."

She eyed him with clear physical intent. "I came."

Only Sherry—and that Helm Lance had to trust but couldn't like. The trial began tomorrow, his ordeal by fire, yet he felt the verities of his life crumbling beneath him. Helm scared him more than the Devil. Both of them seemed so *old.* Lance felt insignificant between them. He wanted to matter, to mean, needed human touch to reassure him. Scheherazade was here and hovering, but the last bedrock principles barred his way with a flaming sword. Let Bakker weaken or Swaggart fall; Candor must not.

And yet Mantovani was playing the love theme from *Ben Hur.* In a wine-warmed surge, Lance saw himself and Scheherazade as torn Judah and faithful Esther. His fingertips reached for hers. "There's so much . . ."

"Yes, Lance. Yes, I'm here."

"So much pain in me tonight. I'm sorry. I don't want to spoil a nice dinner, just I can't help remembering. Did you know?" He forced it out in a broken rush. "Letti and I were voted most popular couple in high school—hey!"

Lance sprang up, jarring the table. Scheherazade saved the wineglasses only by quick fielding. "What's this?" He turned up the TV sound, aghast. "It's Letti!"

Herself, armored in pancake, lashes like rug fringe, talking to Cathy Cataton outside the Hilton.

"—said not to have visited your husband since his arrest."

"That is not true a-*tall,*" Letti brayed. "Not true. Ah have been here time after time, but the government of Coyul and his Satanic minions ruh-fuse to let me see him. But I will be at his side tomorrow, y'all can bet on that."

"No," Lance muttered with a stubborn shaking of his head. "How can she say that? Anybody could visit me."

"True, baby." Ms. Ginsberg was woman enough to know what was good for her. "I've been here every day."

"She's my wife, for God's sake. Why should she lie? Shut *up.*" Lance cut the sound with an angry jab. Mime-Letti turned from Cataton to smile bravely for the camera. Lance rebelled. "No!" Another jab and the set went dark. "No," he grated. Brutalized. Betrayed. Charlton Heston in the Roman galley, pissed off and breaking his oar. "No more. I am sick of her and her eyelashes and her headaches—"

"Right on!" Scheherazade hooted. "Hey, your pizza's getting cold."

Lance eyed her, desperate. Morals warred with elemental needs and lost. "I hope you're not."

"Hell no." She slipped into his arms on cue. "No way, baby."

"A man should hold to what he believes in," Lance resolved, hoping he sounded like John Wayne. "And the woman who believes in him," he added huskily, trying to work the zipper on her jeans. The damned thing stuck.

"Let me do it," she whispered, freeing the zipper. "Love is all that matters."

I will dream the impossible dream, Lance promised himself as the zipper surrendered with promises of its own. Scheherazade unbuttoned his shirt, pressing her leg between his. "We were fated for this. My horoscope knew it," she breathed heavily in his ear. "Let's not make it all missionary, okay?"

"What's missionary?" the sheltered Lance wondered as she pulled him down onto the rug before the fire.

"What you don't know won't hurt us. Oh, Lance lover, am I going to be good for you."

The violins thrilled and sobbed.

At Coyul's salon, the party showed no signs of running down despite the absence of the hosts, which few noticed. The chunky, indomitable Edna had a leonine profile and knew what was good for everyone including Lida Simone, whom she never invited to her own parties.

"Lida, really!"—as Kaufman's leading lady spilled her drink for the third time—"Wouldn't you prefer a bowl in the kitchen?"

"Kinky," Lida mumbled foggily, a pair of dark Foster Grants askew on her surgically reconsidered nose. She had the bedazzled air of one who'd just seen God open on Sinai. "You wouldn't *believe.* I saw Coyul and Purji outside, and I always wanted to ask Purji how she got those marvelous boobs without help. All of a sudden, they started to glow all over"—Lida's expression went ethereal—"like Christmas angels. Then there was just this one big bright light. I think they're making love. Always wondered how they did it. We-eird."

"You are not a healthy person," Edna snapped. "In all my born days —I don't want to hear about it."

Her law laid down, Miss Ferber marched away to take her leave. Lida draped herself along the piano like an arrangement of lilies as Oscar swung into a new number. "I don' know what she's so touchy about. Where's my drink, Oscar? Why are people always stealing my drink?" Lida searched about her. "I didn't see anything you couldn't put in a novel. Even *yours,* Edna!" she trumpeted to the departing author.

"You can tell me," Oscar invited. "My shrink says I need more reality. What happened?"

"*Noth*ing I could see," Lida swore. "Zip. Just lights. Why d'ya think I'm wearing these stupid shades, to avoid autographs? All I can see is orange dots." She found her drink and managed to spill it again. "But they're sweet, Oscar, they really are. Orphans from outer space, jus' like me. I am emotionally starved. What can I do when I am unloved?"

"Quit while you're ahead."

You see? Purji drowsed, her energy and essence one with Coyul's as they drifted under a deep blue blanket of infinity spangled with stars. *You've been with humans so long. Isn't it therapeutic to be home again?*

Truly it was. Coyul felt marvelous, reborn, sinking into the dreamless sleep of his kind.

FELIM TO COYUL: MOST URGENT.

The intrusion jarred them. Purji reluctantly separated from Coyul, reforming in human shape. "The phone at a time like this. Doesn't Felim ever go off duty?"

COYUL TO FELIM: THIS BETTER BE IMPORTANT.

FELIM TO COYUL: PER YOUR REQUEST, CHECKED HELM RECORDS. FORGERIES PERPETRATED BEFORE MY TIME, CLEVEREST IN MEMORY. NO RECORD "PETER HELM" EARTHSIDE OR BELOW STAIRS. ADVISE.

Advise what? Where? The trial of Lance Candor was now a compendium of negatives. A contest not about Candor or his actions, watched by a public more interested in deposing Coyul than exonerating the dense offender, argued by two lawyers not whom they claimed to be and so well disguised not even Coyul could guess their identities.

Felim still hovered in Coyul's mind. ADVISE?

COYUL TO FELIM: BY WAY OF ADVISEMENT, YOU MIGHT TAKE A WILD GUESS AT JUST WHO'S MINDING THE STORE AROUND HERE. GOOD NIGHT, FELIM.

9

Waltz for cobras

CANDOR TRIAL OPENS TODAY
FUNDYS SEE EASY WIN FOR CANDOR
PUNDITS PREDICT PALLID POLL FOR PRINCE

Her tight brunette curls meticulously coiffed, Cathy Cataton faced the cameras outside the Megachurch. In the distance behind her, thousands of people filed like purposeful ants up the marble steps into the grand edifice. Ms. Cataton's on-camera voice, urgent but professionally modulated, gave no indication of being aware she was broadcasting to a sixty share of Topside and Below Stairs.

". . . supporters of Lance Candor say they have no doubt of the trial outcome which will radically affect Topside politics, calling it the most significant spiritual contest in ages. While Fundamentalists are confident of victory, one courtroom veteran said: 'An easy win against Josh Speed is like an easy stroll up Mount Everest.' "

Below Stairs in the Sports Bar, the habitués had agreed that nothing else, not even the Superbowl, would be watched during the trial. This reflected self-interest. If Coyul lost, Topside would become the sort of place to which you wouldn't retire your parents or even enemies. As for Below Stairs, the good times might well be numbered, *were* numbered as far as Arnold Rothstein saw it. He watched the monitor over one end of the bar while Legs the bartender set a fresh drink before him. Legs had once been his bodyguard in the bad old days. They went way back, not without their differences.

"You making book on the trial, Brain?"

"Always ready for some good action." Rothschild tasted the drink, frowned and set it down. "Now I see why Coyul didn't drink here much. You should stock the bar better. Who do you like in this?"

Legs owned to a loyalty bet across on the board on Joshua Speed, all takers. "He's gotta win. Post life will be hell. Death won't be worth living."

Rothstein produced a small notebook. "I say Helm by three lengths. Candor gets off without so much as a slap on the wrist."

"You got a bet." The bartender extended a hand to shake on it. "Joshua Speed is a big man in more ways than size."

Legs had always been impressed by big men, Rothstein recalled, until he figured out how to be bigger. He had the ideal face for a bodyguard or bartender, bland and forgettable. He could move fast and tended to be invisible in any gathering.

"I have a personal dislike for assassins," said Rothstein pointedly.

Legs Diamond didn't even blink. "So do I, Mr. Rothstein. What am I always saying?"

"So you are."

"What's the bet?"

The Benefactor of Broadway thought briefly: there were things he could do without. "If I win, you stop bitching about the *mamzers* who scratched you in Albany. If you win"—the Brain added the faint, deadly smile too well known to delinquent debtors along the Great White Way—"I try to forget who scratched me in New York."

Letti Candor bustled down the corridor to the Megachurch arena, prepared for appearance in more pancake and higher heels than usual. From this moment on, she might be seen on camera at very short notice, and why should Lance hog all the glory? Thanks to God, television and this trial, she had a whole new purpose. Not that she'd take advantage of her husband's hardship, but Burning Bush Books had asked for Letti's life story. She wouldn't think of such a thing except the publisher, that nice Reverend Strutley, asked her personally. He was just like her old pastor back home, strong and reassuring, and when he lit into sin on *tee*vee, you could see him sweat with his holy labor. Letti's fantasies were infrequent and celibate, but in them Reverend Strutley was prominent. He wouldn't bother her with soiled thoughts even though he was a man of the world and even arranged for that tacky little Parker woman to do the actual writing. Letti looked forward to a closer relationship with the Reverend, who already wore white armor in her dreams.

Reality encroached on dream: she was surprised to see Lance approaching from the opposite end of the long corridor and completely unprepared for the female clutching her husband's arm. Letti hurtled forward, her own prehensiles stretching to assert and possess—

"Lay-ance! *Ho*ney!" Letti surrounded her spouse in seconds, pointedly wedged between him and the scrawny young woman with the bad hair job. "Honey, lord am I glad to see yew."

Lance reddened and looked shifty. "Letti. Yes." She guessed he'd try to kiss her like always and braced for an evasive maneuver to save her makeup. When he didn't try, she was sufficiently dense to be relieved.

"Uh, Letti, this is a supporter of mine. Ms. Ginsberg."

"I'm a great fan of Lance's," Scheherazade said with no distortion. "I dig his commitment."

"Pleased t'meet yew, ah'm sure." Letti clamped a deathgrip on the arm relinquished by Ms. Ginsberg. "I guess your fans, won't any of 'em let you alone now, sugar. C'mon, we should go in together. And you, honey"—to the displaced Scheherazade—"y'all should run along and get a seat while's any left."

"Yeah, I better. Take care, Mr. Candor. We're all very much with you."

"Nice to meet yew," Letti threw after the departing fan. "My stars, Lance, that poor li'l thang. Ain't that the tackiest hair job you ever saw?"

"Let's go." Lance extricated himself from her clutch with more than a trace of irritation. "The bodyguards are waiting."

"What you lookin' so mad about? I just said—"

"What was all that stuff on teevee about not being able to visit me? Nobody stopped you."

"I don't know what you're talking about, Lance Candor." Her lashes batted in demure innocence, creating a small breeze. "Ah don't care what all anyone *said.* Ah could not get in. And hell, I been so busy getting ready for today'n going on the teevee. Wasn't hardly a minute didn't have to be somewhere."

"You should have come." Lance pronounced it with a finality lost on his wife.

"Well, shit, I did miss you. Hold on." At the arena entrance, Letti's hands fussed over Lance's hair and paisley tie like two anxious valets. She rumpled his hair slightly to the image from the *Time* cover, tugged at his jacket, smoothed the lapels. "Now you're mama's sweet li'l boy. They're just gonna love you to death. That tacky girl pester you for your autograph or something?"

"Yes, she did." Lance juggled male ego with the common sense of husbands and found a cryptic balance. "And I surely gave it to her."

"That's nice," said Letti.

In a small vestry chamber along the same corridor, Coyul reviewed the line of questioning discussed with Speed and the probable cross by Helm. The ominous murmur outside grew ever louder as the Megachurch filled, surging to a roar as Purji opened the door and came in.

"I wanted to wish you luck before the mayhem. *Bon chance,* darling." She bestowed on Coyul the sort of kiss for which eunuchs might kill. "If we need a getaway, my ship's still there."

"You know I can't. I'm responsible for them." Coyul tilted his head toward the rising thunder from the arena. "Bastards and beauties alike."

"Well, whither thou goest." Purji tried a bright smile, then suddenly squeezed herself tight against Coyul. "Would you hold me? Please?"

"Of course. Frightened?"

"No, just like a human, all of a sudden I feel old and lonely."

"I'm glad you came. Job's comforter. It all ends, you know."

"Small blessings." Purji sighed against his cheek. "Do you honestly think you can tell them everything they know will die, even the universe?"

No, he honestly didn't, but there it was; he was elected. In a thousand or so years, when Earthers had some perspective on space and creation beyond their barnyard world, perhaps the message might filter through. The trickle down theory might better apply to intelligence than Reaganomics. "What's a thousand years?" Coyul lifted her chin, trying to elicit a smile. "We could nap that long."

Purji kissed him again. "When you stop laughing, one could charge you with nobility."

"Bite your tongue. Imagine me hanging next to Washington in the National Gallery." Coyul turned at a polite knock. "Ah, they've even brought the rope. Come in."

The door opened only a few inches; the Prime Minister leaned in politely. "Excuse me, Prince. Just to convey Her Majesty's best wishes. Unofficially, of course."

"Most gracious, P.M. My very best to Her Majesty and Albert in return."

"All in proportion, Prince. She never approved of me, either." The P.M. withdrew.

"Dear old Gladstone. Very helpful though I'm sure he still thinks God is an Englishman. To think: they're going to go through all this over again on Keljia."

Purji sighed. "I suppose so. Next time I'll take along a good book."

"See you tonight, then." Coyul paused at the door, holding on to the miraculous sight of Purji as something sane against the lunacy to come. "I don't think we're humble enough. Nah-h. No way."

"For what, dear?"

"Parents to a messiah."

"We could work at it," Purji hoped. "Didn't I learn French in five minutes?"

"So you did." Coyul blew her a kiss and closed the door. He passed along the corridor with a heavy heart, the muttering of restless predators louder with every step. He climbed the stairs to the entrance and emerged, showing them their quarry. The crowd hushed, vocally crouched, as the mass of them shifted emotional gears. Then a growing sibilance as thousands hissed the entrance of the villain into their sacred melodrama. The few small sallies of applause drowned quickly in a rising tide of boos.

Only a few rose in respect. The first was Joshua Speed. Coyul shook his hand and nodded courteously to Helm at the defense table. Candor's chair was empty.

"Helm's saving him for an effective entrance," Speed guessed.

"Be careful, Josh. That little man with the look of a consumptive poet is diligently sniffing you out."

"What's that supposed to mean?"

"He's out to blow your cover. Make you, as the TV cops say."

Speed studied his huge hands and grimaced. "I'll rely on you to do the same for him."

"If I can." Coyul settled in his chair. "Felim says he doesn't exist."

That was another problem for another day. Speed's concentration focused on the six jurors impaneled in pretrial proceedings. Even with the most altruistic motives, no one came unbiased to the issue of religious belief. From a pool of prospective jurors, Speed had warred with Helm for a balance of attitude. Helm tried for as many hardshell Fundamentalists as possible and all the women he would wangle, knowing them susceptible to Candor's bunting-wrapped personality. He used his peremptory challenges to eliminate, as far as possible, any upper-class or Catholic choices. Speed let himself be guided by Darrow's famous essay on Christian juries. Having the safety valve of confession and absolution, Catholics tended to be more compassionate. Episcopalians could be counted on to be conservative; being deeply invested in the status quo, they would resist all that threatened a comfortable sense of order. Lutherans and the less rabid Methodists were generally solid citizens who wouldn't be hypnotized by charisma but needed to be shown. With Baptists the ground beneath a lawyer's feet grew treacherous, and with Pentacostals he navigated amid quicksand, liable to sink with any step.

Helm got two women, both Baptists, and the flinty foreman, Matthew Wycherley. More accurately he allowed Master Wycherley for the exclusion of a Polish Catholic. Speed managed one Unitarian stockbroker from Connecticut, a Lutheran Swede from Minnesota and a Catholic from upstate New York, an Italian stonemason who looked as if he'd enjoyed his life and hadn't desisted for a little thing like death.

The foreman Wycherley was the only juror not of American birth or the twentieth century, still dressed in the rusty black of his time and place, seventeenth-century Yorkshire. *My own ancestors began not two days' ride from there,* Speed recalled. Wycherley and the two women had the kind of faces Speed had seen and intimately known in river settlements from Cairo to New Orleans. He knew the beliefs burned into them to produce that set. God and life were hard, neither gave quarter to the weak. You were lucky to have a doctor or a preacher within ten miles; more likely you died of the fever or the burst appendix before either could reach you. Someone who loved you washed your remains, dressed you in Sunday best and laid you in a pine-slab coffin. Someone read over you, someone else cut the brief parenthesis of your life, beloved of, born—died, on a raw pine board still oozing sap and smelling of turpentine.

And yet we were optimists with hopes big as the land. Hope was all we had. Despair was death.

The three faces he studied had that same gnarled look. Wycherley came by it naturally, but the women were modern, from a time of television and computers when their well-dressed preachers told them God wanted them to be rich and happy but couldn't quite cheer that flint from their eyes. Hickory people who carved their God from the same fire-hardened wood.

"Hickory gods . . ."

"What?" Coyul looked up.

"Nothing. Just ruminating on juries."

A blast of heraldic trumpets. Coyul thought at first they signaled the entrance of Marcus Aurelius, but the brass went on and on in a flourish Caligula would have thought excessive, followed by a surge and rumble as thousands rose all over the gigantic arena and a brushfire of furious motion ignited around one entry way.

LANCE! LANCE! LANCE!

Without a break the brass swung into "My Country, 'Tis of Thee" for augmented marching band. A squad of busty cheerleaders in sweaters a size too small and emblazoned with LANCE IS ROMANCE, whooped, semaphored, did splits and cartwheels while a leggy majorette twirled and juggled three flashing batons.

WE LOVE LANCE! WE LOVE LANCE!

"—SUH-WEET LAN DUV LI-BURTEE—"

Speed shaded his eyes, disgust silent but classic.

"So much for the majesty of the law," Coyul noted.

"Enter Lance," Speed drawled with a tinge of vitriol. "We are plowing a rocky furrow, Coyul."

Watching the scene on TV, Purji thought—yes, she did see someone in the spectator row closest to Helm raise his arm in a subtle but discernible signal. On cue, so swiftly that cameras had to pan in a blur, a blue-blazered choir of fifty young men and women broke into an up-tempo spiritual.

> Yes, Jesus loves me,
> Yes, Jesus loves me . . .

The song was taken up by thousands, booming through the Megachurch and over the airways of Topside and Below Stairs. The shot cut from the choir to the star of the stampede, Lance Candor, surrounded by six bodyguards. On his arm, Mrs. Candor ogled the cameras like dessert.

Closeup on Lance: Purji could see the sheer gratification in that face. No dissemblance; he didn't perform or play on these people as Helm might. Lance was of them and needed them, basked and believed in the outpouring of their love. A screaming teenaged girl with wild eyes, blocked by a bodyguard, strained to touch even the garment of her god.

And cut to—

The choir leader as the spiritual ended, a clean-cut fortyish man whose Ivy League suit clashed with the smarmy manner of a local TV salesman hawking doubtful used cars. "Isn't it time you came home to Jesus?" he implored the cameras and a million hearts. "After all, that's where you started."

Purji sighed and looked away from the screen. Now and then her eyes suggested not so much vast age as a profound awareness of time and the grain from its ponderous mill. Yet something in her was young enough to protest.

This is dark fantasy. This isn't real. These people are already mastering space, thousands of years beyond the Keljians, but they haven't learned a thing.

The shot cut back to Lance as he strode to the defense table and shook hands vigorously with Peter Helm. As if he'd already won, Purji thought.

What are we doing here, Coyul?

What of all they'd seen in their eons, or that they knew more of the universe now than these people would ever intuit or discover? They were atypical of their own kind—easy, lazing out their ages with laughter as leavening to the pain of awareness. The graceful loving for the sake of love itself, the frivolous bitchery that found pain and passion alike weary givens, the wit that daubed a graffiti mustache of light on the shadowed visage of eternity—what of it? A pretty, pathetic illusion.

These creatures are reality, and in any form, we would be their demons.

There, that was depressing. Purji willed the scotch to hand, a stiff drink in a tall glass. She wondered if George Kaufman was watching. Talk about bad revivals . . .

"All rise."

The crowd rose in perfunctory courtesy when Marcus Aurelius entered. No cheers or applause greeted him. Aurelius wore the late-second-century costume he saw no reason to abandon in post life, a plain undyed linen tunic under a toga of the same natural shade with a single purple stripe to indicate his rank. A spare, modest man, a philosopher king who reigned in a time when a more practical man might have done better, Aurelius was remembered more for his writings than his rule.

"Marcus Aurelius," the clerk droned. "Former emperor of Rome, presiding. This court is now in session."

From the dais raised high above the rest of the court, the magistrate addressed the jury in a voice serene as his bearing. "This is a civil case. You half dozen have a wider latitude than in the mere determination of guilt or innocence. You need only a majority to find for either side or for any degree of damages due the Plaintiff. Herein lies your office, not a jot further. Whatever else has been cried abroad in this case, whatever consequences arise from your decision must not concern you here. You will hear testimony and render judgment on that basis alone. Scribe will now read the plaint and specifications."

The court clerk appeared in closeup on dozens of monitors throughout the arena:

That on the day of his assumption of authority over Topside, Coyul was libeled by the Defendant, Lance Candor, falsely accused of being that entity known as Lucifer or the Devil and by implication inimical to the good of Mankind and Topside.

"He is!" Lance shot to his feet amid a flurry of cheers. He pointed at Coyul with a denunciatory gesture worthy of Hawthorne. "Ask him the better-known name for Below Stairs, that's all." Aurelius rapped for order, but Lance would not be checked. "And you, Judge? You're not even a Christian. I challenge you for bias."

"Indeed?" Aurelius regarded him with equanimity. "When I lived, sir, the followers of your faith were a minor cult who could not even agree on the cardinal points of their own belief or whom they most detested, so-called pagans or each other. If you challenge for bias, I must reprove for barbarism. Sit down, Mr. Candor."

"That's a stupid play," Coyul muttered to Speed. "I'm surprised Helm didn't put a cork in him."

"I'd say he rehearsed it." Speed shot an acerbic glance at Peter Helm. "Don't be surprised at anything you see."

The balding little clerk went on with the specifications of the charge:

That on said date and through the aforesaid libelous confusion of identities, the Defendant conceived of an explosive device, entered without permission on the private space of the Plaintiff and detonated said device, causing grievous distress to the Plaintiff and two innocent parties.

"Counsels will please approach the bench."

Speed and Helm placed themselves before the bench, rangy wolf-hound and lean whippet. "Counsels will remember the emotion surrounding this case and take no undue advantage of these mechanical eyes that enlarge you to the plebes."

"The Elect of God, my lord," Helm prompted softly.

"My definition was considered. Rome, Heaven or Hell, they are a mob capable of being swayed."

"Sir," Helm acknowledged. "How may we address the bench?"

"This being an American trial by American rules of jurisprudence, Your Honor will suffice."

"And less Chautauqua," Speed suggested to his opponent. "That jackass colt of yours pops out of his stall again, I'll move for contempt myself."

Helm stiffened. "For that matter, one could question your own spiritual leanings."

"Enough," Aurelius overrode them brusquely. "I will now hear opening statements. Mr. Speed?"

"Ready, Your Honor." Speed clumped back to his table, studied a sheet of notes and then, over his spectacles, his client. "Worried?"

"Concerned."

"Don't you fret. I've had other jobs but I was real good at this." He removed the spectacles, folding them into an inside pocket.

"Josh, who are you? Just between us?"

"Your lawyer. Best you can get this side of Clarence."

"Thanks a lot. I've got a job to do that I can't even begin until I prove my right to do it. I'd rest easier knowing where I'm trusting my future."

"Sure. See that little bastard over there?" Speed flicked his eyes to

Helm. "I'm his opposite." He moved away toward the jury and stood, rocking back and forth on huge feet, hands clasped behind him, and Coyul *had* seen that stance and heard the voice before, but damn it, *where?*

Speed began in an easy, conversational tone. "My opening remarks will direct your attention to the libel charge and its stain of defamation rather than the violence it generated. Our case then centers on the why of this action. Mr. Candor publicly called my client a demon. *The* Devil in fact, with all the attendant meaning. We will show that Coyul is not and could not be this alleged entity; that he is in fact, as he publicly stated, an alien being from a different galaxy, charged by his superiors to oversee our maturation as a species. We will demonstrate through this that Candor's libel and his violent act retard this actual and wholly benevolent purpose."

Speed paused; his bony shoulders twitched as if reacting to an itch between the shoulder blades. He pulled at one earlobe in reflection. "I won't gloss over the larger considerations of this case; neither will I try to cloud your judgment with grandstanding rhetoric." He jerked a thumb at the defense table. "You'll get enough of that as you go along. Thank you."

Speed ambled back to his place, awkwardly bumping against the table corner. Helm rose but remained in place.

"May it please the court, my remarks to the jury are brief and clear enough that I will address them from here. Defense will show that the Plaintiff is indeed that entity identified by my client, by whatever name, that allegation was in fact truth and therefore the Devil was neither libeled nor defamed, nor in any way distressed by the words or acts of Mr. Candor. As for the larger consequences of this trial, no orthodox mind can accept any other conclusion."

Searching that sensitive face, Coyul for an instant thought he caught a glimpse of something behind the careful mask. Something like a matrix, perfectly built and ordered but flawed by an inconsistency. *And he can't stand it.*

"Further only that you are Christians rendering a verdict on a Christian and a hero who by his actions testified to those very beliefs you hold yourselves. That is all."

When Aurelius addressed counsels, one might have noted an ironic tinge to his words. "I compliment both counsels on their brevity and clarity of intent. And their scrupulous avoidance of emotional considerations while keeping them very clearly in sight. Witnesses are instructed that although there is no applicable oath to be administered, perjury is liable to expulsion from Topside. Counsel for Plaintiff may proceed."

I could lie a little and go home, Coyul dreamed. *The Rock wouldn't be so bad if Purji were there. I wonder if I'm up to all this significance.*

Speed scraped back his chair. "I call the Plaintiff Coyul to the stand."

■ 10 ■

I saw the universe once;
it was closed . . .

Speed had to wait until the boos and catcalls subsided before addressing his first question to the witness. "Your full name?"

"Coyul."

"Have you ever gone under any other name?"

"Not among my own people. Just Coyul."

Speed nodded. He was standing close to the jury box in position to see his witness and evaluate jury reactions. "For the record, would you give us a brief description of your origins and people?"

"People might be inaccurate. *Entities* comes closer."

"I stand corrected. Precisely where do you come from?"

"That's rather involved. If I may, Your Honor?" Coyul asked and got permission for visual aid. The entire ceiling of the Megachurch became a vast electronic map of unfamiliar heavens. "Not as it looks now but when I left it."

An arrow pointed to an E-type galaxy within an irregular cluster. His original planet, Coyul explained, was more gaseous than solid. Sentient life forms tended to be more energy than matter, at least the successful ones. Evolution weeded out the losers but extended survivors' ability to transmute themselves as needed. By the time the planet grew old and started to fall back into its sun, they had long since departed with little need for bodies or physical surroundings.

"The universe was new then; quite new as universes go. We were one of the first of the higher life forms."

Being thus, they considered it a moral and scientific imperative to seed intelligent life by boosting basic potential under strict guidelines and supervision. Within the limits of given ability, life had a tendency to improve and adapt, finally to be aware of itself as in the case of humans.

"So you are essentially a scientist?"

"Not really," Coyul qualified modestly. "Trained as one, but my chosen field is music. Now, Barion had great ambitions in science. That's what started all the trouble. We were still in school . . ."

An older class decided on a graduation party that got out of hand and wandered far off the known universal routes. The party ended on Earth, where Coyul and Barion were stranded for a joke. The problem was that none of the jokers were all that keen at navigation. When they finally got home, no one could remember exactly where they'd left the brothers.

"That was when?"

"About five million years ago. Your Pliocene period."

"Objection." Helm raised his hand. "Aside from being impossible to substantiate, none of this testimony has any bearing on the case."

"Your Honor," Speed retorted quickly, "the case itself arises out of the Defendant's mistaken assumption as to Coyul's identity. I'm seeking to establish that the Plaintiff is an alien life form and where he came from."

"This is not a tidy case at all," Aurelius said. "If you start entering objections on every pretext, we will be ages getting through. Overruled. But counsel will keep his inquiry clearly relevant at all times."

"Coyul, I take it your present human form is an illusion."

Coyul preferred to call it a convention. "I could manage any likeness, but there's the pull of habit."

"For the record, might the jury have a brief demonstration of your native form?"

"Of course," Coyul agreed pleasantly. "If the court has no objection. Don't look directly at me; very hard on the eyes. Right then, here we go."

Even with eyes averted and then shut tight, every post-life human in the Megachurch found the brilliant light intolerable. Television viewers saw their screens become thousand-watt bulbs. They rubbed their eyes —then, through a world of bright dots, saw the inoffensive form of Coyul again. The Megachurch stirred with a vast reaction in which fear and hostility were major ingredients.

"Sorry about that," Coyul apologized.

"You mentioned trouble," Speed went on. "Would you enlarge on that?"

Coyul obliged. He and Barion were young, Barion ambitious and himself rather arrogant. They experimented with the indiginous apes, augmenting their intelligence to Cultural Threshold far earlier than normal. When their own kind found them again, Barion was charged with illegal experimentation.

"I was left here to clean up the mess. As long as it takes."

"Mess?" Helm bristled. "Objection! Are we to understand that human history, its majesty and massive endeavors were considered by his alleged kind to be a mistake?"

"Oh no," Coyul hastily backtracked. "Rather, as Tennyson might put it, a magnificent blunder. Perhaps I should clarify."

"By all means," Aurelius prompted. "I am as interested as counsel."

"Magnificent" was Coyul's tactful addition; the terms used by Sorlij were more pungent. He chose his words carefully now. "If I'm guilty of anything, it is arrogance—a failing ascribed to Lucifer, true, but also to the young of both our races. Barion wanted to do something never done before. I wanted to go him one better. Sibling rivalry."

Only about two percent of anthropoids in the known universe made it as far as Cultural Threshold, Coyul explained, though the species was fairly widespread.

"Objection!" Helm trumpeted. "There is absolutely no way to prove the existence of such worlds populated by men. Not to mention the implied heresy."

Aurelius considered the objection. "Can the witness substantiate?"

"By logic, yes."

"Logic is not hard evidence," Helm objected again. "This is intellectual obfuscation."

Aurelius ruled to let Coyul continue, reserving the right at any time to allow or strike. "Can you by a simple method demonstrate these statements?"

Coyul looked as pained as a mathematician forced to recite his multiplication tables as evidence of qualification. "Will you concede that certain types of soil and climate are beneficial to certain plants?"

So with carbon-based life. Where Earthlike conditions were present, Earth-similar life tended to develop, higher forms emerging when and if conditions continued in their favor. Along the way natural selection went through innumerable random experiments. Man existed on Earth today because, millions of years ago, while the great dinosaurs were stumbling through daylight toward extinction, a tiny warm-blooded creature was clinging to tree limbs in the dark, with prehensile claws to steady itself and stereoscopic vision to judge distance more efficiently than a reptile could.

The root of the problem was that this creature *was* nocturnal. The dark was part of its deepest memory.

"You have never forgotten the dark," Coyul addressed the Megachurch at large. "Even when it ceased to be safety and became a time of fear. Became the evil inextricable from good. You all have it, like the primordial dream of falling that jerks you awake. Even by Your Honor's time, this dualism was an accepted part of religious thinking. The Manicheans, for example, through whom the concept found its way into Christian culture."

More and more dangerous stirrings ran through the crowd. Someone catcalled. From another side came: "False prophets will rise!" Shrill insults fell like rain about the mild little figure on the stand.

"I'm sorry," Coyul said, raising his voice a little to be heard, "genuinely sorry to have to tell you this in this manner. We handled it badly, let things just go on—"

"Devil!" a woman shrieked. "Go back where you came from."

"Madam, nothing would please me more," Coyul confessed. "But I have to finish well what we commenced in ignorance. One doesn't begin a career in obstetrics by assuming discovery beneath a rose bush or delivery by stork. And the cosmos doesn't center on your destiny anymore than your world is centrally concerned with the metamorphosis of caterpillar to butterfly."

"I see." Aurelius meditated for a moment. "I'll allow the testimony. Mr. Helm is overruled. Are you with us, Counsellor?"

Helm's distraction was the Senator from Wisconsin, who had bustled down an aisle to bend over the little lawyer in whispered conference, sliding an envelope before him.

Speed returned to his witness. "I have only one more question, Coyul. How old are you?"

Coyul had to stop and think. "To tell the truth, I've lost count."

"Roughly?"

"Several hundred million years, I suppose."

"Give or take?" Speed's homely features broke in a crooked grin. "Cross-examine, Mr. Helm?"

The Senator's voice was a triumphant hiss in Helm's ear. He vented his manic trademark giggle. "Got it Below Stairs. A few favors called in, a little spade work, and thank God for Roy Cohn."

The envelope contained a single sheet of paper with three names printed in large capitals. All three were recognizable anywhere in the world or post life, except perhaps central New Guinea or the remoter stretches of Siberia. One was heavily circled in pencil.

"Your best bet." The Senator tapped the circled choice. "How's that for a hole card? His wife has been looking for him everywhere."

"Does Defense plan to cross-examine?" Aurelius queried.

"Yes, Your Honor." Helm pocketed the envelope with an approving nod to his associate. "Good work. We should have known."

"We know now." The Senator had never been a handsome man; now he looked positively malevolent. "I don't know why *he's* hiding out, but you can stop him cold."

As Helm approached the witness stand, Coyul reaffirmed his first impression of the man: the nineteenth-century notion of a poet in appearance; beneath, a graceful dancing snake.

"You said you have no name other than Coyul among your own alleged kind."

"I was given no other name," Coyul testified.

"Although others have been ascribed to you, such as Prince of Darkness?"

"Yes."

"And after that demonstration that blinded the eye but not the mind, I recall that you have also been known as Lord of Light."

"That too," Coyul admitted. "Lucifer, Tempter, Adversary—all equally unflattering and inaccurate."

"Inaccurate? A moment ago you stated that the cosmos did not center on Man's destiny any more than this world was centrally concerned with caterpillars." Helm delivered his zinger to the jury and audience.

"To a Christian viewpoint, that is an inducement to despair, which would neatly fall into the Tempter's suzerain, so far as he was able. Would you deny that?"

So far as he was able: there it was again. Veiled as Speed, Helm still leaked readable meaning to Coyul. Again he detected conflict in the man, as if something in his own logic would not quite mesh gears. *God's will supreme, the Devil powerless without it.* Yet for all the conflict, a formidable and obsessive strength of purpose.

"Does the Devil deny that?"

"Objection."

"Sustained. Mr. Helm," Aurelius cautioned drily, "play not so obviously on the plebes. This is all very strong wine for them."

"Very well." Helm took the rebuff with gritted teeth. "Does the witness deny that?"

From stubborn Speed: "Question leads the witness."

Not at all leading, but Speed, bless him, wasn't giving a free inch anywhere. While the bench considered its ruling, Coyul's mind went on-line to Felim at Records Retrieval—

COYUL TO FELIM: QUERY PROGRESS PETER HELM IDENT?

FELIM TO COYUL: NEGATIVE LAST THREE CENTURIES. STILL CHECKING BUT THE INFIDEL DOES NOT EXIST.

COYUL TO FELIM: HELL HE DOESN'T. KEEP GOING BACK. ECSTATIC SECTS, ALL VARIANTS, EVEN MANICHEANS. I NEED TO KNOW WHERE THIS VERY DANGEROUS LITTLE MAN IS COMING FROM. DIG, YOU PERFERVID RUG DEALER.

FELIM TO COYUL: ACKNOWLEDGE. MAY THE FLEAS OF A THOUSAND CAMELS BITE AND AFFLICT YOU.

COYUL TO FELIM: HAVING WONDERFUL TIME. WISH YOU WERE HERE INSTEAD OF ME.

"Your Honor," Speed asserted, "Defense is laboring to put a certain color and wholly unwarranted construction on my client's testimony."

"And you have not been as diabolical?" Helm flared at him. "You have put a civil case that requires such questioning, introduced a cerebral and secular line of examination which I am constrained to follow in cross. My compliments, Mr. Speed. However, in this welter of cerebrality, let us not forget *my* client or his motives, which mirror those of every Christian in this church."

Helm paused for the scattered cheers. Home viewers saw the cameras cut quickly to Lance Candor, unfortunately discovered picking his nose.

"Mr. Candor is a Christian Reconstructionist. The question reflects on his deepest beliefs and the actions derived from them."

"I find the witness's responses troubling myself," Aurelius confessed. "He will answer the question."

"Yes," Coyul responded. "In some it might induce despair. In others perhaps art."

"And therefore be consonant with the Devil's intentions?"

"That construction might be—"

"Answer the question as put to you. Is it not so consonant?"

"I suppose it is if—"

"Thank you. You have described your brother Barion as a scientist who brought certain apes to—I believe you called it—Cultural Threshold. Would you enlarge on that term?"

Cultural Threshold, Coyul defined, was the point at which an intelligent species began to adapt environment to itself rather than the other way around. Stone tools, for example, which in turn further developed the brain toward even more complex invention and culture. A benevolent domino effect.

"I see. And you allege that you and Barion created humans out of these apes?"

"No." Coyul passed a hand over his eyes, weary of spelling out the intricate shorthand formulae of his own culture. "We took a pre-human creature and simply accelerated a process already in motion. With good or ill result, depending on your view."

"At which time you were already in disagreement with your Lord—excuse me, your brother?"

"I was as responsible for the experiment as Barion, even more so. I corrected for his error in the effect of oxygen on the cortex. In any case, without boosted intelligence, the subject would never have survived the predictable rigors of the environment."

"Never have survived?" Helm's eyes lit with opportunity. "I'm sure this honorable jury notes the heresy wrapped in scholars' terms. From God's ultimate creation to an ape unable to survive without the aid of alchemy. I put it to the witness and this jury that this alleged noble experiment is no more than a clever misrepresentation of the rebellion of Satan against God; that in any Christian country the author of such heresy would be jailed or even hanged." He impaled the foreman with his eyes. "Even yours, in your time, Master Wycherley."

To Helm's surprise, the jury foreman answered firmly in his Yorkshire burr: "Not without fair trial, he would not. You could not say that of Spain."

No profit there; Helm left it quickly and brought the focus back to Coyul. "Do you deny that you speak heresy?"

"Mr. Helm, you are tedious."

"Witness will answer the question," the bench directed.

"How? It's apples and oranges, a divine scenario against physics and chemistry. Nature plays no favorites."

"More heresy," said Helm.

"I was there," Coyul tried patiently. "Intelligence is selective but nature is random. Like a shotgun from which, out of a hundred pellets aimed at distant possibility, one might hit. Most will miss. In the case of anthropoids, ninety-eight percent."

"May we inquire of your expert knowledge how we fare against other such experiments?"

Watching at home, Purji knew the look on Coyul's face. When truth is useless, be kind.

"Because you were CT'd much earlier than usual," Coyul began cautiously, "you are the toughest and most adaptable of your species in the universe. And among the most technologically advanced." Also the most violent, but that wouldn't help his case just now.

Helm bowed slightly. "You honor us. Though the jury and this Christian assembly would hardly consider that paramount."

"Not bad for openers, Mr. Helm. Or for survival."

"Then surely, from your vast cosmic experience you must have gleaned some spiritual comparison as well. Or would you consider that insignificant?"

"The spiritual. That is a problem."

"I daresay, for you."

"You're not the worst."

"We are relieved," said Helm over a groundswell of catcalls.

"Your Honor?" Speed requested and got a moment of private conference with Coyul, towering over the Prince in the witness box. "He's already brought in the tinge of heresy. No matter how you answer, he'll twist fact to these dimensions."

"He said it, Josh, I didn't."

"Flies and mules, boy. Flies you catch with sugar, not vinegar."

"There's too much sugar in their spiritual diet already. Diabetics. You know what I've got to do."

"I know something about mules," Speed maintained. "Helm is one. Behind all that articulate logic is a belief in the totally illogical."

The man was right—and so *damned* familiar. That high-pitched, twanging voice was on the very tip of memory. "All right, Josh. I'll be as sweet as I can."

Speed sat down; the clerk repeated the question.

"You are the most spiritually passionate humans I've ever encountered."

"Praise!" Helm turned out to the crowd at large. "From one present at the Creation, who graciously admits our natural aspiration to the Elect of God!"

A tidal wave of applause greeted his triumph, whistling and cheering, drowning out Speed's futile objections and Aurelius pounding for order.

"Order! Order! Peace!" But the faithful would not be quelled. Only when Helm raised a restraining hand did they begin to subside. The subtle shift of power felt ominous to Coyul.

"Be silent or I will clear this court. Counsel for Defense will hereafter address himself to this court, not the plebes, or I will find him in contempt."

That contempt and the power he felt conferred on him by the audience was audible in Helm's retort. "My apologies. Your Honor." He moved to face Coyul again. "I am nearly finished with this witness. I put it to him that this alleged experiment is a tissue of lies; that Man was created by God in His image and that you as His rebellious servant could not, for all your perversity, make one move without His willing it. But you tried, didn't you? Your gracefully admitted responsibility in that Creation was to make Man fall. Isn't that right? *Isn't* it?"

And Purji, watching Helm on the home screen, thought: *No wonder I love the Charleston. With so long to live, it's love and dance or go mad.*

"You seem hesitant, Prince; one might say loath to answer."

Coyul answered with more sadness than subterfuge. "Simply to deny says nothing. I'm not your Devil, Mr. Helm. You insist I am because you must. All of you."

"By all means: in simplest terms." Helm smiled tolerantly for the jury's benefit. "For our limited understanding."

"In American terms," Coyul said. "Some years back there was an American fad for something called past life therapy . . ."

A number of "therapists" made a good living from sounding the subconscious thoughts of romantically inclined mediocrities for the kings, queens, swashbucklers and conquerors supposedly lurking within. One impartial psychologist observed at the time that the human psyche was always full of old B movies, though it was a fun way to redecorate an otherwise unremarkable life and harmless as playing Monopoly.

"An age-old longing among your kind, Mr. Helm. Carl Jung called it the collective unconscious."

By which were meant the myths that explained not the human mind but the deepest heart and that enduring darkness present from the beginning. Oedipus, Osiris, the dying and reviving gods, the Grail, Judas and Modred, Loki, Grendel, the dark urge to entropy, the fall of Man, of Valhalla, of Satan himself. Great quests, great stirrings, great betrayal and loss—all painted in vivid primary colors. The conflicts and undying ideals of the human spirit.

"This states the condition at its best, Mr. Helm. The human soul is a passionate pulp writer, dramatizing Fall and Redemption in a script that makes you the star, when the moment of Creation and Fall were simultaneous, no more—and magnificently no less than the terrible beauty of knowing you existed for a little and would end, and your myths the hack-written product of a mind that will ever put what it feels above what it thinks or sees. Are these understandable terms?"

"Indeed," Helm acknowledged, more subdued. "They are eloquence of a kind."

"I was there."

"And yet we are *here,* Prince." Helm uncoiled and struck. "By whatever name: Heaven, Topside, Hell or Below Stairs, we did *not* end. We continue. Only the Devil could so malign the majesty of Creation, and only the Devil would. We are *here.* Perverse as you are, can you not see the hand of God in that?"

"You are perverse!" Coyul snapped back at last. "You and your kind of human that take your transient lives and make them sterile with groveling and guilt. Take the warm little light of a shining intelligence in a dark place and let it die from guilt and fear."

"I repeat—" And yet Helm was surprised by the sudden power out of that soft, near-epicene figure on the stand. "In our own immortality, do you not see God?"

Coyul hesitated, weary of Helm, ages of him. "I have been tempted to look for the entity you call God in many places. Hoped for Him, dusted for His prints, but never found them except perhaps in men and women who rose above themselves to say *we* instead of *I* before they died of neglect or were crucified. Immortality is a loose term, sir, inadmissable evidence. There have been other post lives from other worlds. They passed away as their last energy dissipated. This world, this galaxy, this single breath of the universe will exhale into the next. Even me, Mr. Helm, and the cosmos will neither mourn nor even remember me. I am not depressed by the prospect."

"By Heaven's very gates," Helm swore to the jury. "Can we not hear in this *passive* lie the vindictive agony of the Pit?"

"You wanted simple terms," said Coyul. "American terms. There's a saying in Poker. 'If there's only one game in town, you might as well play.' "

11

Ladies of the hour—

"It's the 'Ricky Remsleep Show'! Starring that underground favorite, RICKY REMSLEEP! Co-author of the new Topside musical *Kingdom Come,* with music by George Gershwin. Ricky's special guest, Scheherazade Ginsberg. Now, here's Ricky, so let's GET IT ON!"

Yay! Crazy! Do it!

Amid the raucous welcome of his audience, Ricky Remsleep stepped out of the studio wings, denimed and leathered, guitar slung at the ready. The studio was packed as usual with his tireless following, flower children who had overdosed no later than 1970, anachronistic as a reunion of Confederate veterans. Ricky knew his people and his time. The guitar was an old twelve-string. *We came first with the truth,* his alienated defiance told the camera. *Dig it or fuck off.* Ricky banged out a chord on the twelve-string. "Whatta you got, Brown Shoes?"

"WHATTA YOU GOT?" his groupies bellowed back.

"BROWN SHOES!"

Their ragged chorus behind him, Ricky hit another chord and belted his trademark tagline. "WHATEVER YOU GOT, WE'LL FIGHT IT WHILE WE CAN!"

He moved to a tall stool, fingering the guitar as the applause subsided.

"Okay, outa sight. I'm with my own people." He picked out a seventh and diminish. "You've all had your minds bent with this Candor jazz. Just want to mention my famous collaborator, a cat by the name of Kaufman, George S. Case you children don't remember, he's from the time when we all did corn flakes in the morning. Real B.C. Well, we're getting our show on, but there's a language problem, and I've been giving old George some hands-on training in relevance."

He rippled out a few soft chords.

"Got a real down girl coming out now. Maybe some of you heads remember her from our own time of peace and love. Let's lay a welcome and good vibes on—Scheherazade Ginsberg!"

The polite applause surged to enthusiasm as his guest bounced out of the wings to her camera marks. Scheherazade's sense of costume was equal to the occasion: hair a startling burnt umber, braided and held with Apache beads, full buckskins decorated with Thunderbird motifs. She wore soft calf-length boots and an elaborate belt of Mexican silver around her thin waist, both hands aloft in the V-sign of peace and love, smiling with that half-innocent, half-sardonic manner perfected by Joan Baez that said to a whole generation: *We are refugees from our own culture.*

"Let's do our thing!" she sang out.

"Right on," said Ricky.

"And if nothing else is beautiful or real, we are."

"Tell it like it is." Ricky motioned her to the guest stool. "You people, maybe some of you got straight enough to catch the Candor trial on the tube. Don't put it down too far because Scheherazade has something to say."

Perched on her stool, one booted foot hiked on a rung, Scheherazade pointed to the studio audience, collaring them verbally from the start. "Listen. I know Lance Candor. I was there demonstrating when they took him in. He's a man with a soul and a mission. Let's do it, then. Let's get out and be counted for Lance."

Watching the program with a concentrated Joshua Speed, Coyul had to laugh in spite of himself. "I've always thought of Ms. Ginsberg as an unguided missile."

Speed kept his eyes on the screen. "Candor's been bundling her."

"Bundling?"

"She's been coming to dinner and staying for breakfast."

"Been snooping, Josh?"

"Oh . . . courtesy of the night desk clerk at the Hilton Hereafter. Fellow named Bixby. I got him off a death sentence once. He's always been grateful."

"Useful."

"Not half as useful as she might be."

"I wouldn't trust her to be a coherent witness."

"Maybe not," Speed mused over folded hands. "But the very hell of a hole card. You saw what Helm did yesterday with the audience. He's beginning to control them." His deep-set eyes flicked up to Coyul. "Ever see a lynch mob work themselves up into a real Christian mood?"

"Hey, man." A bearded and bellied youth in a dirty T-shirt and denim vest rose to rebut Scheherazade. "Don't put us on. This Candor dude is white bread from the Bible Belt. We ain't a bunch of fuckin' Fundys."

"Get straight, man," Scheherazade went back at him. "Ricky remembers the Movement better than you do. There was peace and love, yeah, and down with Dow Chemical and all that, but some of you got into Jesus, too. Remember? Fuckin-A you do. Lance is a fighter for a *cause*. You gonna turn off on him because he ain't Abby Hoffman? Fuck you, man."

She bounded off the stool and spiked on her camera marks again.

"Look," Scheherazade gave it to them straight. "Lance is a Fundy, sure. A Christian Reconstructionist. But he's counterculture like us. Don't let the squares cop all the tube time. Stand up and be counted for a revolutionary. Gonna be some changes. Yeah!"

She jabbed a finger at a soulful young girl in a flowing red moo-moo who had risen, weaving a little. "What's your story, girl?"

The girl spoke in a foggy lisp. She seemed to have trouble focusing her eyes. "I just wondered, like I'm very heavily into astrology—"

"No shit?" Scheherazade forgot all else at mention of the sacred. "Me too. I live by it."

"Too much," the girl enthused in a sibilant rush. "What's your sign?"

"Triple Scorpio."

"Oh, what a conjunction! Like *2001*."

"Speaking of that." Ricky made a bid to get his audience back. "I was rapping with George Gershwin the other day—"

"Talk about history," Scheherazade jeered. "He was back before the Stones even."

Another girl bobbed up from the front row, spaced out and all of sixteen. "Let's do the I Ching!"

"Crazy!" For Scheherazade, Ricky, the show and causes were forgotten. "Uranus is in my sign and I got a feeling the changes are gonna be like awesome."

Sharing diet cola and doughnuts in bed (she had warned him often on the dangers of coffee), Lance and Scheherazade turned on the TV the moment they woke up, the way a smoker would reach for his first cigarette as a matter of course. They re-ran her guest segment three times before idly switching channels, coming in on a florid commercial.

"Sherry? Look at this."

An illustrated book cover zoomed out of the distance straight at Lance.

THE HERO'S LADY
by Letti Candor

The commercial had nothing if not production values—urgent, breathless, overshot and scored for several massed symphony orchestras. They might have been advertising perfume. Lance felt sick.

"Sherry, look."

She did. "Jesus *shit.*"

"Don't talk like that."

"No wonder she never had time to visit you."

"Sherry, I swear to God I didn't know anything about this."

She found his crotch under the covers and patted it. "I know, lover."

On Earth the commercial would have cost millions: an idyllic scene of a boy and girl running in slow motion through a green field.

MALE VOICE-OVER: They came from the American Heartland with a dream, a faith . . . and a date with destiny.

QUICK CUT TO—

A man aiming a pistol at the President. ACTOR LANCE diving between them. ACTRESS LETTI SCREAMING PHOTOGENICALLY. CUT TO—

ACTRESS LETTI (with an accent never farther south than Staten Island) in tearful close-up, tortured but defiant: "My husband died a hero! If the state of Kansas won't admit that because of his faith, God *will*."

—as the shot cut in a triumphant welter of strings to a simple but dignified funeral, then ACTOR LANCE running toward ACTRESS LETTI over a field of pink clouds.

VOICE-OVER: A love story that has lasted beyond death. (DISSOLVE TO BOOK JACKET) *The Hero's Lady* by Letti Candor. Her own story, available now from Burning Bush Books.

FEMALE VOICE-OVER: Reading it is an act of love.

"So's a vibrator," Scheherazade razzberried through a mouthful of doughnut. "And it's more fun."

Lance stared at the screen, confused and hurt. "So that's where she's been."

"Come on, who cares? I went on the tube for you too, didn't I?"

"Writing a book." Something like informed disgust adulterated Lance's innocent mien. "Letti couldn't write a check."

"It's cool, okay?"

"This makes me feel—"

"I'm here." Scheherazade slid her hand under the covers again to stroke his thigh and adjacent attractions. "I'm here, baby."

Lance moaned and buried his face in her breasts. He felt lost in a quicksand swamp of Helm, Speed and duplicity that now included Letti. The world was sinking under him. "Running across pink clouds . . ."

"That part was kind of nice," Scheherazade remembered wistfully, slithering out of her pajama top. "I mean, if we could do that sometime without being square, you know?"

"Reaffirm me," he gasped, clutching at her. "Validate me. Right now."

Through an endless series of commercials, Scheherazade validated the bejeezus out of him.

"It's the 'Georgia Grieves Show'!"

Applause. The cameras panned over the studio audience full of older women in hats and a sprinkling of captive husbands. Timing herself expertly into the ovation, Georgia Grieves, *soignée* and tailored, strode out to face the studio audience, lifted her arms in greeting, then took a seat on the small podium as the camera cut to—

"Georgia's special guest—Letti Candor!"

In the guest chair, Letti smiled directly into the camera.

"And Mrs. Candor is here today to tell us about her new book."

Letti held *The Hero's Lady* upside down as Grieves named the title.

"Which will be on the stands in about five minutes; isn't that right, Letti?"

Letti giggled. Her makeup wrinkled slightly. "That's right, Georgia."

Grieves removed her glasses, habitual when she wanted to get down to it just between girls. "You've written an absolutely riveting book, Letti. I absolutely couldn't put it down."

To be accurate, she couldn't pick it up. A production assistant skimmed the volume and wrote a short synopsis which Grieves studied for five minutes before air time. "Did you write it with anyone?"

"Well, I did have a li'l help on things like English and spelling and how to put down mah ideas," Letti allowed demurely. "It was all just comin' out so fast."

"Ye gods and small fishes." Dottie Parker turned off her TV in disgust and swore with a facility undimmed by death. She poured her first scotch of the afternoon, her eighth for the day. "Jus' comin' out so fayast. Horseshit. Which is spelled with an *e*, madam."

Dottie finished most of the scotch in one practiced pull. "Oh dear, that does soften the pain. How are the mighty fallen," she mourned to her poodles, "and how the appalling become mighty."

She was sorry she had agreed to ghost the miserable book, except she had to cure her writer's block some way. Beyond that she had always been, dead or alive, a world-class masochist.

Back at celebrity, Letti was telling Georgia Grieves and the cosmos at large of her husband's ordeal. Joshua Speed, she asserted, must have been a carpetbagger while he lived; she knew the look and the breed. Letti became noticeably more "Southrun" as she progressed. She spoke of her idyllic life with Lance, the joy they found in life and the Hereafter, of their faith. She struggled with and then surrendered to copious tears, blotting deftly with tissues, then went under again in a fresh convulsion. Disinterested watchers like Coyul were amazed at her flow of tears and how little damage such monsoons had on Letti's mascara. Her diction might falter but her makeup was from the Alamo.

"When . . . when ah think of what that awful Speed will try to do to mah husband on the stand. Why he don't even go to church, I hear. Just a trashy, awful man in the employ of the Devil."

Passing fresh tissue, Georgia observed with left-handed admiration, "It's wonderful how your makeup doesn't even run."

Letti gulped, gasped and blotted. "Ah use Ever After." She showed most of her upper plate in a plucky smile broadened by her confidential agreement with Ever After to do their next produced commercial—which, she was assured, would be as major as the one for her book. Her nice Reverend Strutley had an interest in her and also Ever After.

"We'll be right back—after this."

CUT TO SPOT COMMERCIAL: Ever After, the post-life pancake that keeps you looking almost alive in his eyes.

"That woman is connected to Great Salt Lake," Coyul marveled over his sushi. "I haven't seen that many tears since the Republicans lost to Roosevelt."

"For all her agony, she made sure the book stayed on camera." Purji's normal expression, that of a slightly erotic angel, was now rather curdled. "Lord. Someday my wonderful Keljians will come to this and call it civilization. Don't you get discouraged?"

"Tell me about it." Coyul pointed with his chopsticks. "More hamachi, dear?"

12

—And a nice girl from out of town

Cathy Cataton considered death a distinct improvement over life in relation to news gathering. There was no practical reason to bar TV crews from any Topside trial. The bad news: she and her board man, Benny, had to share the press box with Nancy Noncommit from Below Stairs. She wondered if the dyed-blond bitch had been born with that surname or had won it through her deadpan delivery on camera. Cataton had other appelations for her BSTV counterpart, all descriptive. She disliked Nancy from her questionable red shoes to her sprayed hair. Cataton's hair clung to her scalp in short black curls, an ingrained habit from the long wearing of a wimple. She wore a headset now, giving muttered directions to Benny and her cameramen on the floor.

"Everybody stay sharp. Superbitch is here. We don't want to look bad. Camera one, stay on the witness box. Two, on the lawyers. Three, you hang loose to go anywhere on my signal, but punch up a good shot of Candor on my cue."

Benny's nasal voice whined in her headset. "What about Coyul?"

"Only if there's nothing else." Cataton put a tiny lighter to a Virginia Slim. "Who needs him?"

"You think he's the Devil?"

"Get serious. He's a wimp."

"So who is, do you think?"

"I'm a convent girl." Cataton winked at him. "I cannot tell a lie. It was me all along. Heads up, guys, they're starting. Camera three, get the judge. Everybody ready? Benny . . . go."

"Ladies and gentleman," Speed commenced with the jury, "I've demonstrated through direct testimony that Coyul is a still-living member of an alien race and therefore could not be the entity Lance Candor intended to and did attack, inflicting needless distress. If you feel this contention well proven, my case is won on the spot. However, I won't ask for a premature verdict. As corroboration, I will present a witness of Coyul's own race and long acquaintance. I call Purji to the stand."

As he spoke her name, Purji appeared like sunrise in the nearest arena entrance.

The rustling audience went silent, not with their usual hostile tension but an emotion less easily defined. They saw a slender young woman of about twenty-seven in a simple white garment that suggested the Age of Fable, lustrous golden hair falling over her shoulders halfway to her perfect waist. She walked from the entrance to the witness box. She did not slither, swing her hips or exaggerate the progress at all, but every male in the audience felt something of a coronary flutter. The natural motion of that body was ineffably feminine, a definition of the gender. For those mysogynists who died at ninety and would rather burn eternally than be young again, there was something achingly familiar in that fluid movement. They had loved her once or dreamed of it. Their ideal of Woman, near-forgotten in atrophied libido, walked new as spring, possible, attainable.

Viewing from his bed, one octogenarian nudged the white-haired mate of an unromantic lifetime and gummed lasciviously, "Gimme m'teeth, Martha. I want t'bite you."

In the arena audience, distaff reaction was distinctly biased. "Goin' round in something I'd be ashamed to wear for a nighty," Letti disapproved to her friend, Bernice. "I declare I can jus'bout see through that tacky thing."

Males were not so detached. Romans and modern Italians yearned to pinch her sculpted bottom, Greeks pondered a new lexicon for desire. English Puritans damned her on the spot, Jews felt pleasurably guilty, Fundamentalists knew she was something to be given up on principle.

Lance Candor regretted she hadn't gone to his high school. Athletic and educational nights with Scheherazade had widened his appreciation of life as an enjoyment. The arena seemed faintly perfumed with fragrances associated with spring and poignant memory.

Coyul winked into Purji's mind as she stepped into the witness box. *Lovely, dear, but don't overdo.*

Joshua Speed was careful not to block the appreciative view of the Italian juror. "Your full name is Purji?"

"Yes."

"Where were you born?"

Her response duplicated Coyul's for the question. "But it's not there anymore. Nothing lasts, you know."

And how old was she?

"Oh. I'm terrible at birthdays." A hand fluttered to her brow. "Three or four hundred million of your years. I'm a little younger than Coyul. We went to school together. Coyul, Barion and I."

Uninterested in Coyul, the cameras missed his smile hidden behind one hand. He remembered Purji being somewhat older—and distinctly felt her frown into his recollection now. *Don't be ungallant, darling.*

"Have you ever gone by any other name than Purji?"

"Not among my own people."

"I see."

"Of course, the Keljians—"

Purji, shut up.

She caught herself. "I did visit for some time among the Keljians. They called me Lua-lat."

Coyul glanced over at Helm; the lawyer was jotting a note.

"You were not sent there by your own people?"

"Those stuffy old academics?" Purji's laughter tinkled through the arena like lightly tapped crystal. "Catch them wasting time on humans." Anthropoids were fashionable with her own generation for a time and a passion with Barion, unfortunate since he apparently bit off more than he and Coyul could chew between them.

"Of your knowledge, then, neither Barion nor Coyul ever considered or represented themselves as deities?"

"Barion? Oh, that's funny." A fresh spate of giggles took Purji. "He was very young and enormously impressed with his own theories, certainly with his lapses into poetry—I understand your Whitman adores him—but no. Never in his most self-congratulatory moments did Barion ever think of himself as a god."

Speed persisted. "Did Coyul ever think of himself as such to your knowledge?"

"Coyul is a musician." Purji's amusement turned tender as she smiled at her beleaguered friend. "He would dearly love to hang a DO NOT DISTURB sign on some remote corner of the Void and just compose. As for being a god or a demon, as you conceive of them, neither vanity is in him."

"No more questions. Thank you."

"A moment," Aurelius interjected from the bench. "Are we to understand that you consider godhead a human vanity?"

Purji's brief hesitation represented a synthesis too rapid for most computers: an answer comprehensible to a second-century Stoic. "Among the best of humans, the concept of good for its own sake is an ideal. Among us it is a given."

"A very good answer," the magistrate considered. "As for vanity, certain of my imperial predecessors allowed themselves to be deified in life."

"Lifetime is the key," Purji said. "Yours span less than a century, ours close to a billion years. That's a long time to cherish illusions, Imperator."

"Yes. I've dropped a few in the last thousand years myself. Proceed, Mr. Helm."

Purji tried to read Helm as he approached the witness stand: masked as efficiently as Speed. One had to go by surfaces. In the pale blue eyes, flecked with hazel and malice, she could read passion like a concentrated flame but nothing warm.

"You testified that to your knowledge, Coyul never represented or considered himself a god, is that not true?"

She had so testified.

"When did you arrive here? Only a few weeks ago, wasn't it?"

"Yes."

"Being elsewhere in the cosmos for considerable time, you weren't in contact with Coyul for many ages: is that not true?"

"That is true."

"Then your statement as to his personal attitude and ambitions toward godhead are based on former acquaintance rather than current knowledge, am I correct?"

Purji was forced to admit that as well.

"And the former emperor of Rome, our present judge, himself admitted that one or two of his predecessors accepted the honors of divinity before death. I won't dwell on that except to note that power is an open door to such temptation. In your former testimony, you implied that you went under another name than Purji on an alien world. Would you tell us that name?"

"They called me Lua-lat."

"And they were called . . . ?"

"Keljians."

"Thank you and please bear with me," Helm appealed pleasantly. "I am more interested in this sojourn than my colleague. For myself and the jury, would you enlarge? When did this occur?"

"In Earth terms, about six thousand years ago."

And how did she come there?

"I was what you'd call a dropout from my society. Bored, looking for a little fun."

"Lua-lat," Helm repeated the name. "Interesting. These Keljians are human?"

"Very human. Among the most beautiful of your kind."

"Names usually have a root meaning in any language. What is the meaning of Lua-lat?"

"It means spirit of love."

"Spirit of love," Helm echoed for the jury and spectators. "And you were among these lyrical creatures six thousand years?"

"Yes, I was."

"A prolonged visit."

"Not at all by our measure."

"By any measure. What kept you there?"

"The people and the climate are lovely."

"Please. Spare me a disingenuous reply. What status did you hold among these folk?"

"He's going to gut her with this," Coyul worried to Speed. "Can you object?"

"She mentioned the name in direct testimony," Speed regretted. Too late he realized his original idea to use Purji as an expert witness on godhead would be vulnerable. He had switched to plain corroboration of Coyul's testimony, but Helm picked up on her verbal slip about the

Keljians. "She'll have to get out of it by herself, unless I can find valid objection."

Tell the truth, Purji, Coyul flashed into her mind. *But don't volunteer anything.*

"I'll repeat the question," Helm said. "What status did you hold among these Keljians?"

"They looked on me as a fertility goddess."

"A fertility goddess. Well. Despite your earlier testimony that Barion and Coyul modestly eschewed such titles?"

Purji tried to regain lost ground. "You must understand—"

"I do, madam."

"The timing, the mindset when I arrived. They'd just begun to suspect, as your primitives did, that men had something to do with childbirth. For ages before that, women were a mystery, producing new people from their bodies every now and then. Women were therefore believed to have powerful magic working through them."

"May we not be precise and call it witchcraft?"

"Objection," Speed broke in. "The witness is stating a commonplace of modern science that Counsel may have missed in his headlong rush to militant faith."

"Missed? The implication is naked!"

"Not so bare as your ignorance. Your Honor, must the court send Mr. Helm back to school for common knowledge before he is competent in this case?"

"The implications of testimony seem as obvious to me," Aurelius ruled. "Witness will answer."

"If you wish to use that term," Purji conceded. "They'd just begun to grasp—no, let me rephrase that. What I described was part of their stone age—much longer than yours. Gradually they linked sex with childbirth, but the connection between women and magic as a popular notion lingered on. They considered *me* magical, appearing and disappearing at will. Gods always reflect the needs and nature of the worshipers. Keljian kings envisioned and carved gods like those of Egypt, a very sophisticated pantheon. The common people had more immediate needs and fashioned much like your own peasants. The need of men and women for each other became an integral part of faith. Sex meant children, children meant strength and prosperity. I filled a need, Mr. Helm. I never considered myself a goddess, but they did. The vacancy came up, as you might say, and I took the job."

"And allowed yourself to be worshiped as a pagan deity."

"Object to the word 'pagan.' "

"Sustained."

Helm whirled on Aurelius to protest. "Your Honor—"

"Counsel will allow my authority on this point."

"Not without the taint of bias."

"With none, sir. As *amicus curiae,* friend and informant to the court record. The term 'pagan' has no relevance where there is no established orthodoxy. In my own time," Aurelius pointed out, "your faith was considered a radical cult. The pejorative use of 'pagan' arose only as your cult prevailed."

"With all respect"—though Helm's tone grudged it— "Your Honor may not understand all that is at issue here."

"On the contrary." Aurelius did not bother to conceal his weariness with the self-evident point. "Sustained. Get on with it."

Helm swallowed his irritation with visible effort. "You allowed yourself to be worshiped as a deity?"

"I'm afraid so," Purji acknowledged.

"Which would hardly seem beyond the fell clutch of vanity—also noted in conversation with the bench. As for filling their need, one can readily believe you an inducement, if not to fertility, at least to procreation." Helm turned out toward the spectators and the television monitors. "Were you not in fact little more than a temple prostitute?"

Generally bored by the dry stretch of academic definitions, the audience came awake with new interest.

The term escaped Purji at first. "Temple . . . oh yes. Your ancient Babylonians had such a custom. No, my function was different."

"How?" Helm pressed in on her. "Did you not copulate with Keljian males?"

"Of course; that's part of the job."

"Would it not be accurate to say: with any male who desired you?"

Purji struggled to gear her mercurial and vast mind to his narrow line of attack. "Chosen males at chosen times. Why do you harp on—?"

"By any definition, weren't you a glorified prostitute? Not merely, as you so blithely suggest, a tourist off on a lark, but a whore. In fact, the Great Whore!"

Cresting a tide of applause and vociferous agreement, there came the flat, unlovely voice of Letti Candor—

"That's what we'd call her in Kansas!"

The timing as much as the sentiment evoked a burst of laughter from all quarters of the Megachurch. Aurelius pounded for order as the derisive flood refused to abate. "Order! Silence, I say! This court has authority to close the hearing to spectators, and so it will if—"

"You may *not.*" Helm turned on Aurelius, pure vindictive steel. "This is the House of God. You may not close this place to any Christian soul. You *will* not."

Applause and cheers greeted the challenge as the court clerk conferred with Aurelius in hurried whispers.

"The court is reminded that Counsel is correct. I may not remove anyone from this place." Another flurry of cheers mixed with more pointed sentiment. Aurelius waited them out, choosing his words with care. "Defendant has already implied that I might be biased against him. I refer Defendant and his counsel to the distinction between religion and cult as they were understood in the Roman Empire during my reign. That empire no longer exists in any legal sense, therefore objection to bias is as invalid as any lingering imperial attitude, and the jury is so reminded. The court is less biased toward either side of this contention than any judge from any Christian sect could hope to be. I may bar no one from this place, but if it is necessary to the dignity of these proceedings, I can and will change venue and hear the remainder of this case in the Void."

The damper was effective. In the press box, Nancy Noncommit hissed into her headset, "Shit, that's all we need." She hated any trip across the Void, no matter how brief. No one wanted to be out there for any time or any reason. Aurelius gave the house at large time to meditate on the alternative before motioning to Helm.

"Counsel may proceed."

"Object," Speed drawled. "Use of the words 'prostitute' and 'whore' prejudicial."

"Question arises from testimony," Helm rebutted very much as Speed knew he would.

"Overruled, but Counsel will show the reasoning of his interrogation."

"Your Honor, my reasoning derives from the most ancient basis of Western faith, the Hebrew texts. Purji, are you not in fact the Arch Whore herself? Lilith, the very demon and embodiment of lust?"

"Oh, Lilith." Purji's brows elevated in recognition.

"I thought you would recognize the name."

"Yes, I learned Hebrew this morning. Thought it might help. Lilith is . . ."

"Yes?"

"A very primitive concept."

"I would say basic."

"The Hebrews borrowed her from the Assyrians. Not only a rebellious demon of lust, but rather inconsistently a destroyer of children."

"Come now," Helm snapped at her. "If the dark is part of us, as Coyul said, then surely there can be no good without its counterpart evil, as no solid object can stand in sunlight without a shadow. This also is basic. Do you deny that you are Lilith, the embodiment of lust, rebellion and destructive jealousy as Coyul himself is the Devil?"

"Of course I deny it. I've already said—"

"Not Adam's first partner in lust? The very uncontrolled spirit of abandon itself?"

"Objection!" Speed was on his feet, an angry edge to his prairie twang. "Objection!"

"And I object to your continual harassment with pointless interruptions!"

They faced each other, the rest of the court forgotten. Noncommit and Cataton pained the ears of their technicians to catch every second. Noncommit hadn't caught live stuff this good since the fascist leader Roy Stride got a juicy tostada in the face and his erstwhile girlfriend called him an asshole for a fifty-share of fascinated post-life viewers. Helm knew the cameras were on him and played to them now. "Let all of this go in the record," he demanded.

"Damn you, you little—"

"Counsel for Plaintiff is out of order!"

"I don't have a word for you, Helm. The witness has testified she's an alien—"

"Alien as any demon!"

"You're trying to blacken her with a naked appeal to ignorance and superstition."

"Order!" Aurelius commanded. "Counsels will both come to order before I hold them in contempt."

"By *God!*"

Coyul blinked open-mouthed. The lurching, clumsy Speed had suddenly become a monolith before him. *"Put* me in contempt then. *He's* the hanging judge with this primitive cant and spurious dragging in by the heels of medieval metaphysics. By all that's decent and holy, Helm, I'd like to put you on the stand and ask what glorious chapter of the Inquisition you illuminated."

"None, sir, but for such great purpose—"

"For God's sake, man. Can't you conduct yourself like a gentleman?"

"Gentleman?" Helm appealed the proposition to his audience for its sublime absurdity. "Is that all you can bring against me, all you can weigh against my holy cause; that in a matter of such eternal pith and significance, I am no *gentleman?*" He dismissed the suggestion with utter contempt. "Christ my witness."

"This is heaven," Cataton glowed. "Stay on them both. I love it."

"The Devil himself has been considered urbane," Helm seethed. "As he sits here before us, certainly I can find no better description. Chivalry? You ask such hollow considerations of me when I confront the greatest lie of the ages?" Helm's voice broke with his effort. "Here in this tormenting place where the faithful find not the City of God but only this ambiguous limbo, venal and mundane as any earthly wallow? You charge me with bad manners when the cosmos cries out for one answer and this *creature* on the stand defiles everything that—" Helm halted mid-thought, trembling. "Let me tell you plain: I have broken such things as her on the rack and would again. I call on Christ to witness I would put my own flesh and blood to torture for such a cause, even my own body, purifying my means by their holy end."

"As did the Inquisition!" Speed slammed back at him. "Your Honor, I apologize to the court for my interruption and remarks. The censure of Counsel's tactics is your province, not mine." Speed clumped back to his table, muttering to Coyul as he sat down, "How'd I do?"

Coyul was surprised. "You mean all that was calculated?"

"Oh, my heart was in it. Also my method." The church was full of Americans. One thing Americans had always suspected were Europeans and their influence. One thing the common people always aspired to —and Speed came from their heart—was to be ladies and gentleman. They might deny it in an egalitarian flush on the Fourth of July, but the old yearning was there.

Helm could only accede with as much grace as possible. "My apologies as well, Your Honor."

"Thank you . . . gentlemen," Aurelius accepted with an acerbic smile. "Nice of you to return the court to me. One more outburst from either of you and venue removes to the Void."

"Defense withdraws the question out of deference to Counsel's fragile sensibilities."

"That's white of you," said Speed. "Can you spare it?"

"Please don't withdraw." Forgotten in the flurry of emotion, Purji enjoined Helm. "I would like very much to answer the question."

"It is withdrawn," Aurelius instructed her. "You need not."

"But I would, Imperator." Purji's smile made Aurelius momentarily forget his Stoicism. "Mr. Helm's question reflects a deep faith if not a profound understanding, and deserves an answer."

For the benefit of the jury, Helm noted, "One cannot fail to note that Lilith and Lua-lat sound suspiciously alike."

"Or lily," Purji reminded him. "A flower associated with the resurrection of your Christ. The similarity of sounds from one language to another is a shaky argument, Mr. Helm."

Furthermore he had repeatedly mentioned "the uncontrolled fire of lust" by which she assumed he meant the dangerous female principle uncontrolled by worried males, implying that it must somehow be controlled. Another commonplace, predictable when the human mind tried to separate spirit from flesh, calling one holy and the other impure. The old dichotomy of light and dark, chaos and order.

Listening to her, Coyul remembered saying as much to Barion when they stood over that flea-bitten ape at a Pliocene waterhole. *But no, you had all the answers.*

"In this unnatural schism," Purji went on, "the very heart of religion becomes schizophrenic. What you call pagan rites are as much a part of the process as what replaced them, and with a valid truth of their own. Forgive me." She massaged her temples to ease the strain. "Among my own kind so much of this is expressed in accepted formulae, it's hard to conceive of anyone debating it. The people, the poor, always have a sharper sense of reality, living so close to it. Mostly they were the poor who came to me for their marriage rites. Dazzled when I blazed on my altar and then descended among them in flesh. They built the temple and the rites were theirs, prized by them. They brought loaves baked from the best of the little grain they could spare, fruit from their few trees, even roast meat from their own herds, barely afforded but never grudged on a wedding day. Now and then their masters might eke out the feast with leftovers and feel complacently virtuous, much like yours.

"The brides and grooms looked very much like the new-married poor anywhere: stiff and formal, shy, eager, a little foolish. Stunned by being important for a moment, wearing their garlands as if these colors and fragrances would be with them always. Most never wore flowers again. Like your own poor, they worked themselves to death and died too young though they no longer looked it. But for that one day they all got a little drunk, made love in the spill from the bride's joy, and I could see in their eyes that one day's respite like a victory from all the grinding days to come, none of them brighter than yesterday.

"Such lives are not poetry, Mr. Helm, but for that one day at least they found all the rhyme they could ever keep for themselves and knew all of God they could ever understand, and that enough. They believed in the goddess because they could touch her. She blessed their unions and a lucky few men loved her in glory for a night before working themselves into the grave.

"Then the priests of the new religion came, as they always do, and told them God was never a woman but a stern, punishing father; that their guilt was obvious and their joy unclean. All so predictable, Mr. Helm. I may be frivolous, but somewhere in an unguarded century I came to love them, and I carried that love away with me. I hope this answers your question about the purview of goddesses."

"Most moving," Helm said with a glance at his audience. They were attentive and still, impressed though he could not gauge how. "The Devil himself could not have put it more convincingly. I have only one or two more questions for Lua-lat. Obviously you and Coyul are scholars. Would that learning be inconsistent with diabolical intent?"

"Objection!"

"Oh Speed, desist," Aurelius squelched him wearily. "This has been a trying session and I'm heartily sick of you both. Defense will get on with it and make an end, I hope."

"Please the court I will do so," Helm promised, "and even rephrase. Since Purji is conversant with our religious history, she will recall the lucid explanation by Tertullian of pagan beliefs: that these rites, however gross and imperfect, were practical exercises designed by God to bring men gradually to the true faith."

Purji was familiar with the facile explanation and the author should have blushed. "That's like a milliner saying that heads were clearly designed for the wearing of hats, as your Voltaire remarked."

"To mention facile arguments," Helm parried. "Voltaire is a supremely entertaining atheist. One final question then: if you could succumb to the lure of godhead, for all your ages and superior intellect, is it not possible that Coyul, by whatever name, could be so moved to indulge himself?"

"I've already told you—"

"I know that, but I ask is it possible? In the early eras of this world, could he not have been tempted to let mortals think of him as a deity?"

"No."

"Not possible when you indulged yourself? Appearing at will in a blaze of light, enjoying worship. Not *possible?*"

"That isn't in him."

"Will the court instruct the witness to answer? I am querying possibility, not disposition."

"Witness will answer."

"Is it not possible for him when it was clearly possible for another member of his alleged kind? Regardless of his statements?"

"Yes," Purji was forced to admit.

"Thank you." Helm spun on his toes and walked away with a dismissive gesture. "I have no more questions for this erstwhile goddess."

"Witness is excused."

All eyes were on Purji as she walked to the nearest exit. Only one voice broke the silence, the piping curiosity of a small child. "Mommy? Is the whore-lady going home?"

Helm waited out the resultant laughter, then observed, "Out of the mouths of babes."

"If Helm weren't so passionate a man," Speed grated, "I could easily despise him." Helm controlled the spectators, not himself—that was clear. A quick jab under his guard was needed; *hit him where he ain't.*

Aurelius inquired, "Does Counsel for Plaintiff plan to call other witnesses today?"

"If Your Honor please, a moment." Speed murmured to Coyul. "Right now we need heavy artillery. I've had a notion from the start and Helm has just told me how right I was—for once. Trust me." Speed half rose to address the bench. "Your Honor, since my next witness will require some time to appear, Plaintiff requests recess until tomorrow."

Helm appeared suspicious but could put forth no material objection, and Aurelius was clearly relieved. Court recessed.

"Josh?" Coyul asked. "Who are you going to call?"

A contented grin threatened Speed's outsized ears. "Helm's got the crowd on his side. Time I complicated his life a little. He said let Christ be his witness. All right, I will."

■ 13 ■

Mister Godot won't come today

"How are we doing? I mean honestly?" Lance asked after they'd taken their places at the defense table.

Helm didn't look up from his notes, small, precise jottings on tiny cards. "We have the people with us. If they are indicative of the jury, we've already won."

Lance didn't feel much better. Asking assurance of Helm was like warming your hands over a block of ice.

Helm would not share his deeper thoughts with Lance anymore than he would converse with a house cat. He had told a part of the truth. The rest was that Speed worried him. He hadn't expected yesterday's resistance, nor did he believe for an instant Speed's theatrics were any less calculated than his. Purji had gone defensive; no one in the audience but knew what she was. Speed's ploy and his incessant objections were meant to delay and obfuscate. But surprising. Helm would not have credited him with so much fire.

Helm had tentatively decided on a few witnesses of his own but discarded the notion after seeing his *fils d'un chien* of an opponent at work. The American term was more puissant: Speed was a tough son of a bitch. Amazing that such a quality should have been overlooked in a man who was derided in his own time as a buffoon.

Helm thought of Augustine as a witness: a gutter fighter in debate, but Speed was no complacent Pelagius to be laughed out of contention. Erasmus was too much of a humanist to suit Helm, Thomas More too Catholic and above all as English as the jury foreman, Matthew Wycherley. French-born, Helm had always considered "English" and "enemy" synonymous and distrusted them from pure instinct.

Spiritually treacherous bastards. I never understood them. Who could? Exactly three hundred years after me comes Speed, American but wind-blown from the same English weed, poisoned with secularity. God himself would not trust them. Did not Henry Tudor, in my own lifetime, make himself Supreme Head of the so-called Church of England? If Speed presses too hard, I will unmask him. That is my weapon.

Helm would have called God to the stand but didn't delude himself about the possibility, though he had thought to summon Christ—another maddeningly elusive figure difficult to find as an honest lawyer. No, the popular support he leaned on wanted spectacle, not rarefied debate. He would let Speed select witnesses and then demolish them as he had Purji. As for Candor, he already had the sympathy of the crowd and could be tutored for the stand.

All rose when Aurelius entered and settled himself on the dais. "Is Counsel for Plaintiff ready to proceed?"

"Yes, Your Honor."

"Again I caution both counsels that this court will tolerate no more outbursts such as we were subjected to yesterday."

"Your Honor, I stand reproved." Speed's lanky frame unfolded joint by joint from the chair. He rummaged his pockets for a crumpled note, smoothed it out then lurched across the open space between his desk and the jury. Before he spoke, Speed let his deep-set eyes rove over the expectant audience. In the press box, Cataton nudged her board man, Benny.

"Who does Speed remind you of?"

"Henry Fonda."

"Get serious. Fonda's a hunk."

"I am serious. Henry Fonda."

"What are you doing in television, Benny? You can't see a damned thing." She turned to catch Nancy Noncommit bumming one of her Virginia Slims. "Hey, Noncommit?"

"Hey what? You're always smoking mine."

"Look at Speed. Doesn't he remind you of someone famous?"

"Yeah. An ugly Henry Fonda."

"Forget it."

"Perhaps I should apologize to the jury for my part in yesterday's display of temper," Speed began. "During that outburst, my colleague said, 'Let Christ be my witness.' Very well. My next witness has known the Plaintiff for two thousand years. I call Yeshua of Nazareth to the stand."

The name meant nothing to most hearers for an instant until they made the connection. The audience gasped as one person, strained forward, many rising to see or twisting around toward the nearest monitor. No one appeared in the usual entrance or simply materialized as Purji had. A slender young man, casual in an old sweater and slacks, simply rose from the first row of seats and walked to the witness stand.

"My God." Cataton studied the closeup on her monitor. "He looks like a Pakistani cab driver on Third Avenue."

Hardboiled for all her convent training, she found the image on the stand difficult to meld with lifetime habit. True, the thirtyish young man was taller than most Middle Eastern types but the main problem for her, and most of the other watchers, was generations of bad religious art that romanticized the features, moving their cast steadily northwest of Judea to something comfortably Anglo-Saxon.

"I've seen him around for years up here," she realized. "Never paid much attention. Talk about low profile."

"That's him," Nancy maintained from more recent acquaintance Below Stairs.

Cathy Cataton was shaken out of her natural rivalry with Noncommit. "Jesus, why didn't he *say?*"

"Say what?" Nancy crushed out her cigarette and checked the polish on her nails. "Look, you're the nominee at the Republican Convention. The people's choice, great white hype, the whole nine yards. You gonna get up and tell them to forget it, you're really a Democrat?" She turned away with a smirk. "Camera three, pan the house. This ought to be good."

"The fantasies I've had about *him,*" Cataton told her assistant through the headset. "When I was a novice with the Sisters of Perpetual Agony."

"Was that their real name?"

"Should've been. Number three, get off Candor. Get the house. Find some sweet old lady with tears and make her a star."

"Object, Your Honor."

"Alas, Mr. Helm, whatever for?"

"This witness is obviously a fraud and a blasphemous one at that."

Marcus Aurelius passed a hand over his brow. "We had a difficult time yesterday. Let's start at least in cool blood. You'll have your chance."

"State your name for the jury," Speed began.

"Yeshua of Nazareth."

"Known to Christians as Jesus?"

"In Greek and Latin texts, yes."

In close-up on the monitors, the young man did not look at all god-like. The eyes flashed with intelligence and there was more than a hint of strength in his stillness. Beyond that he might have been a member of the Hagganah or indeed driven a cab in New York.

"To be specific, you are the person called the Christ?"

"Another Greek word," Yeshua defined. "I am the person they thought of as the Christ after my death."

"How long have you known the Plaintiff Coyul?"

"Since before I died."

"Would you explain that please?"

"Coyul came to me twice in my life, once when I began to speak as a rabbi. I didn't understand what he said to me, but told my fellows about it. They misconstrued that as they did so much of what *I* said, then and afterward. He came again at Gethsemane." The quality in the compelling voice was not bitterness but its white ashes. "Far too late then."

Speed moved closer to the jury. They and the audience were unusually still. He couldn't tell if they were stunned, reverent or about to attack. "Did Coyul or Barion ever represent themselves as gods?"

"Never," Yeshua responded with a slight shaking of his head. "They became the best friends I had in post life, maybe the only ones."

"That surprises me, sir."

"Why should it? They were all disappointed in me. I could see it in their eyes. Saul, Augustine, even men who went to the block in my name, like Thomas More. Mrs. Eddy called once but left after ten minutes. Joseph Smith . . . he should have written fiction. What an imagination. A few Catholics took me up gingerly, then dropped me like something too hot. The Christ meant certain things to them, a certain image. Not me. Barion and Coyul were a comfort. So old. Seen so much of it before."

What did the Plaintiff tell the witness concerning his own origins?

"That they were left here through a prank that grew into a condition. That's true; only a little while ago they took Barion back. He tried to keep things efficient, so did Coyul. Neither of them had much sense of organization. Pilate would have made a better god figure."

To himself, Coyul ruefully admitted that truth.

"Let me ask directly, then." Speed addressed the question as much to the jury as to Yeshua to measure their reaction. "Did you consciously establish a new religion?"

Yeshua thought about his answer. "No. How do you create a faith when you build with human spirit and its memory? These are always more conventional than visionary."

Speed examined the faces of the jury. The stockbroker seemed troubled, both women shocked, Wycherley attentive but skeptical. The Italian was dozing.

"This isn't the first time I've been asked," Yeshua told Speed. "I'm a Jew. I have my people's passion for a personal God, and that was what I was trying to find again. The faith of my people had become as sterile as yours is now. Rome wasn't our worst enemy, we were. From a people defined by holy law, we had become one crippled by it. The letter of the law crushed out its spirit. As for messiahs"—old agonies passed like a cloud over the contained passion in that face—"they came out of the desert every month, crying for one solution or the other, usually a return to the old ways, much like America today. The old ways weren't gone, but *there,* smothering Judea. I spoke in their terms to their need and passion for God. It was Saul who took it to the Gentiles, that garment so ill-fitted and piecemeal that they've been tailoring ever since. There's more Greek thought and Roman politics in Catholicism than there is of me; more German deliberation in the Lutherans, more uncomfortable compromise in the Anglicans. Now and then someone sensed the truth behind the dogma and got crucified for it.

"Do you understand? Under the dust of dogma settled on my own faith, I tried to find the direct, personal covenant between God and men. They asked me then and for years after Golgotha: was I the Messiah?"

Speed put the question quietly. "Were you in fact?"

"I was one of them," Yeshua answered simply. "Not born of a virgin or a miracle, but—"

He had to wait until the sudden restless reaction in the Megachurch abated. "What is a miracle, Mr. Speed? Any of you; what do you think of as miracles? Perhaps it's a miracle that a child can come bloody and squalling from his mother, unable to speak or think beyond feeding, yet grow tall enough to conceive and challenge the infinite. Isn't that a miracle? My conception of God was no better than my human sight. But I still believe. It's like that play Sam Beckett wrote, *Waiting for Godot.* The world waits as it can, with patience or without it. Despairs, threatens to give up and leave, yet waits on. And every day we're told that Mr. Godot won't come today but surely tomorrow. And believing it or not, we wait."

Watching Yeshua with vast admiration and love, Coyul remembered what Nietzsche had once written, that the struggle for freedom must be fought not only without fear but without hope. Some perverse electron in his makeup kept hoping the German was wrong. His glance flicked idly to Lance Candor: a very atypical expression for that naive young man, not so much intelligence as complacency disturbed and unable to rearrange itself.

"So I have kept to myself," Yeshua concluded, "and gone on waiting."

"No further questions, sir. Thank you for coming. Your witness, Mr. Helm."

Before Helm could rise, the nasal insult came out of the crowd like a handful of garbage hurled at Yeshua. "Sheeny! What you tryin' to sell us? You ain't Jesus!"

The burst of laughter was more released tension than humor, but Yeshua didn't even blink as he looked up at the hostile sea of faces. "I wouldn't try to sell you anything, mister. You already chose Barabbas."

When Helm approached the witness box, there seemed to Coyul more deliberateness in the lawyer's manner, a slower tempo of movement and thought. Failing to find any record of "Peter Helm" anywhere, Felim had collated available parameters from Helm's statements in the trial record. Being a Moslem, Felim was totally objective, even casual, about Christian matters. Coyul had in his pocket a sheet of paper much like that furnished Helm by the diligent Senator from Wisconsin, but more detailed.

ASSUMING HELM STATEMENTS TRULY REFLECT MINDSET, COULD NOT HAVE FLOURISHED BEFORE CA. 1450 OR LATER THAN 1700. BETTER ODDS PROTESTANT THAN CATHOLIC.

Followed by a roster of names encompassing the entire thrust of the Protestant Reformation. Zwingli was first on the list, followed by Luther, Melancthon, Erasmus and others. Felim had circled Zwingli's name as best bet. The zealous son of Islam had done some unsolicited plumbing on his own. At the bottom of the printout was a confidential message to Coyul in Arabic—

DRANK WITH MARK TWAIN LAST NIGHT. CERTAIN IDLE STATEMENTS REGARDING ARTEMUS WARD CONFIRM YOUR THEORY IDENT "JOSHUA SPEED."

"I know," Coyul told Felim privately. "I've remembered him now. And you'll forget."

"Except that proof would entail a trial in itself, I would challenge your alleged identity," Helm stated flatly to Yeshua. "I do challenge it. I must."

The little lawyer appeared more controlled than ever, as if fighting for that rule within himself. The fact didn't escape Josh Speed. "Whatever I did," he muttered to Coyul, "I did it good."

"If you wish," Yeshua said, "I could appear as in life. With or without the thorns, Mr. Helm?"

"Don't be facetious!"

"I am not."

"That hardly helps confirm your alleged identity."

"You miss the point. You heard that sentiment from the crowd."

"I apologize for that man," Helm amended quickly with open scorn for the insult's author. "He should be removed."

"The House of God, remember?"

"For whom you still wait. But why, Yeshua—why, if you are truly the Christ, the gatekeeper for God's predestined saved—"

"I told you—"

"I know. Even if you were not born of a miracle but only predestined as a link between God and man—"

"Predestined?"

"Why did you not proclaim yourself here?"

"I've already said why," Yeshua explained. "No one believed me. No one wanted to believe me."

Helm's reiteration was a razor. "I said *proclaim.*"

The notion faintly amused Yeshua. "Again you miss the point. Like that fellow up in the seats there, they couldn't handle my being Jewish. It's always been a problem, having to share a Testament and a God with us when for so long they managed to keep us out of the better neighborhoods. Not joking, Mr. Helm. We were a small, wandering people who needed a God who could travel light on our way to milk and honey. An omnipresent, invisible God."

Helm rejected that. "You're avoiding my question. Why did you not announce yourself here?"

Yeshua protested; he did not avoid at all. Barion, for all his failings, ran a democratic Topside. One could believe as he pleased, but no one could proclaim anything as theological dogma. Barion had ruled that out starting with the Egyptian Old Kingdom when religion became truly complex.

Yeshua rested his elbows on the lip of the witness box, smiling patiently at the lawyer. "You'll find that's true of democracies. They're never as tidy as absolute rule, and even the asses have a right to bray. Proclaim? So little of what I meant is in your churches. I was an embarassment to avowed Christians and irrelevant to anyone else."

"Permit me to echo a commonplace," Helm said. "Without faith in miracles and the inexplicable will of God, there is no religion, merely an ethic. Would you agree?"

"Readily," Yeshua nodded. "I have my people's need for God, even though the Jews stood more on obedience to God's word than wonder at His miracles."

"Be that as it may, where would the world be without God's will or His Salvation?"

"I don't know," Yeshua responded candidly. "For myself, such a lack is unthinkable, but you might pose the question to a Buddhist or Taoist, where it becomes even more interesting. Without Christianity—your European form of it—there would have been nothing to stop Islam when they swept up through Spain. Without that fervor that pervaded every breath of Northern life, the West might well be speaking a kind of hybrid Arabic today. The Moslems had an equal religious passion, a code of morality more rigid than yours, more abstemious laymen, more learned teachers, more passionate poets, a far higher standard of sanitation—and were courteous enough to consider me a prophet."

"You only reaffirm my faith," Helm maintained.

"And my own." Yeshua smiled. "It's an old Hebrew trait to consider the other hand. Is fact so dry in your mouth that you need magic to wash it down? Barion could have given you miracles; that would have been so easy, to be the apparent god you hunger for, to mouth the comforting lies you need to hear. He was better than that."

"Are you better than that?" Helm jabbed. "Do I detect a bitterness, a disillusionment in you?"

"As a man, yes. I thought I was right. As a spirit, I'm still waiting. Man will always wait and always believe. Faith is alive, faith is life. Faith is a passionate singer, a lark at morning, a nightingale under the moon. Man's need for God is as urgent as his need for a woman." Now the smile was indeed bitter. "A sweaty, living fact that Saul and Augustine, Jerome and Tertullian were ever uncomfortable with, that need for relief in flesh as well as spirit. They wanted to choke that life out of faith. They're doing it in America today when they proclaim that God speaks through this fool or that televised zealot and no one else. You've mentioned heresy in this trial. *I* was a heretic, Mr. Helm. What else should they do but nail me to a cross for it?"

The young man turned his hands over and studied them with a dark memory. "Miracles? Want to see the wounds, Mr. Helm? No trick to that, ecstatics have produced stigmata for centuries. The miracle would be all of you understanding who I was and where I fit into an ongoing process. The tragedy is, perhaps you never will. You'll do the same thing again and again to anyone who disturbs your illusions about God and makes you actually think about Him."

"As Coyul is crucifying Lance Candor for *his* beliefs." Helm swung around to confront the jury, his arm flung out to his client. "Who did no more than you alleged, tore away at old, rotted and unsafe laws and present lies." Helm pointed now to Coyul. "This rabid cur slinking loose through the City of God—"

"Objection."

"Sustained. Colorful but hardly germane," Aurelius ruled. "Constraint, Counsel. Clerk will strike that from the record."

Stricken from record but not from Coyul's memory. He unfolded Felim's memorandum, crossed out Zwingli's name and circled another choice. He must be getting old not to have caught the nuances before this. The city Geneva, the man himself the churning white-hot heart of radical Protestantism, whose views made Luther seem like a conservative pope. *What he couldn't have done with television then. His descendants were just waiting for it like the Hittites for iron.*

"Where did Candor's motives differ from your own?" Helm challenged Yeshua. "Alive or dead, what did he desire but that same clearer definition of and union with God?"

Yeshua appeared weary, no longer interested in the questions. "Candor's motives are his own. I never argued the need for secular law on Earth. You might even recall something I *did* say about Caesar's due."

"There is no law but God's. There can be none!"

"You seem to be finished with me," Yeshua inquired civilly. "May I go now?"

"Finished?" Out of that small, dynamic figure came a desperate gesture of both arms, all the stronger for having escaped his tight rein. "I have no further questions for this witness."

The slim image of Yeshua simply faded from the box. Helm addressed the court. "Your Honor, let—let the record show that I would bring a charge of perjury against the witness were there time or proper circumstance. However, I do request a moment's recess to confer with my colleague."

The bench granted his request. Helm moved to Speed, and bent over the table, intense. Only Coyul heard their exchange. "No matter who you are, Speed, no matter how once revered, may you be damned as a blasphemer for eternity. Do you intend to put Candor on the stand?"

"Wouldn't you?"

Helm's eyes narrowed. "We need to talk before that."

"Oh?" Speed leaned back in his chair, which definitely felt just then like the catbird seat. "Bargaining a plea, Counsellor?"

"I know who you are." The statement dropped like a heavy stone. "I could tell them all right now. They'd be fascinated, especially your wife. I want a conference. Oh, come," Helm reasoned, "you're no stranger to compromise. I loved the City of God, you the image of a state, and both of us sold out whatever we had to for them. Is there any more blood on my hands than yours? Conference."

Speed looked down at his big, misshapen hands. Coyul saw the homely features constrict in pain. "Where?"

Helm relaxed a little, feeling control back in his grasp. "Why not your Void? In your agnostic manner you seem drawn to it."

"Being an agnostic is like being a Thanksgiving turkey," Speed drawled. "I'd be somewhere else if I could figure a clear way out."

"We need to talk."

"That ought to be interesting." Speed tapped his folded hands against his lips. He rose to address Aurelius. "Your Honor, both Counsel for Defense and myself request recess until tomorrow."

"Your reason, Mr. Speed?"

"My colleague and I agree the preparation intervening will be fairer to my next witness."

"Granted. Court stands recessed until tomorrow."

Speed winked at Coyul. "All right, you're on," he said to Helm. "See you in the blue." He vanished out of the chair and the church, streaked through a jumble of conceptions that blurred like subway stations past his consciousness and shot out into the infinity of the physical universe.

14

Two views from the summit

Speed surrendered like a swimmer in gentle swells to the vast motion of the universe. Below, the blue-white ball of Earth turned lazily in space, the moon a pearl on black velvet. Above the dull brown carpet of the Sahara, a tiny point of light: a satellite inundating the world with information.

When I was born, you couldn't send news faster than the fastest horse. Then came the miracle of an electric spark that could flash across the continent in an hour, if the Sioux didn't cut the wire. That satellite, with chips smaller than a fingernail, can shower earth with information automatically sent and received in bare seconds. What do you call a miracle, Mr. Speed?

Miracles came, astonished for their moment, became commonplace, but always with the first wonder came the fear that Man had wrought more than he could manage, and the cry for return to simplicity.

Until we managed as we always do. Our timidity is exceeded only by our courage and curiosity.

Here in the Void, Joshua Speed came as close to articulate prayer as his complex, shadowed mind could frame, always more awed question than comforting belief. He watched the small figure of Helm come closer, somehow inimical to this place.

"Evening, Helm."

"I hope you didn't wait long."

"Not at all. I like it here."

"Yes. You would."

The galaxy turned imperceptibly; they turned with it. Speed could feel the discomfort in his opponent who hated this place but would not flinch from it. Some men never sat a horse well but wouldn't quit trying.

"So you know who I am. Seems your disguise is better than mine."

"My name is not so readily conjured with," Helm conceded with sardonic modesty, "but your Puritans carried my beliefs to Massachusetts and your Fundamentalists are reviving them today."

Speed's knowledge of history was more instinctive than academic. "German?"

"French, from Picardy. A lawyer like yourself."

"That much in common at least."

"At best, except that for any man living through any age, it is always modern times. You spawned in the vigor of a new country, I in the rubble of the Middle Ages. Labels are misleading and posterity always smug. In the sixteenth century we thought our times as post-modern as Reagan's. Why should we not? Our verities seemed as bankrupt, the theology of Rome venal and desiccated fustian. As in your time, tradition no longer fit. Don't underestimate me."

"I haven't so far," Speed said truthfully. "For a while, keen as you are, I thought you were Luther."

Helm shrugged with concession. "Luther argued well, but for all his revisionist cant, he remained Rome's vacillating lover, half gone yet half stayed. The eye that offended *me* was plucked out. I went back to first principles and created a pure theocracy *there* on Earth for the Chosen, the Elect already separated from the goats by God's wisdom and His Grace. As they did once in your country; as they are doing now because mine is the one ultimate, irreducible faith for the common man."

"To America's discredit," Speed said with a rime of distaste.

"Oh, listen to him. Listen! The syphilis of secular honor." Helm's hard laughter echoed in the Void. "Does it discredit a drowning man to clasp himself to that which cannot sink? Jesus, man!"

Speed thrust deftly under the other man's guard. "Speaking of whom."

The yearning in Helm told Speed he'd hit home. The Frenchman stared out at red Mars and distant Jupiter with bitter defiance. "Do you think I can accept that man as Christ?"

"That's why you're here, isn't it?"

Far out in space two titanic meteors collided in silence and burst apart, fragments streaking like tracer bullets through the upper atmosphere of Earth. Helm pointed. "There's your reality. Your ethic. Do you imagine all men are like you, that they can look on the blind, brutal collision of events and believe in no more than an equation? You think I can accept this . . . indifference?"

"Yeshua shook you, didn't he?"

Helm was turned outward toward space, still defying the equation. "It *is* indifferent. It crushes me. Even if he were that martyred mortal and Christianity the ill-fitting garment made from misunderstanding, yet it was made and covered us. He admitted that. I would rather believe a lie of faith than the reality of this Void. If Yeshua spoke truth, so did I. Without faith in what we cannot see or explain, there is no religion, only mutable ethic."

"Are you afraid of that?"

Helm shot Speed a poisoned look. "Oh yes, I'd forgotten. Your legendary image as a man of the people. Speak of lies. You were never of anything but solitude."

True enough, Speed knew. Not even his wife got that close to him.

"Great sorrows were attributed to you," Helm went on. "The maudlin turned you into suffering Christ. How did you deal with that suffering? As when your son died. Did you share the grief with your wife then? Did you share hers?"

"I tried." *No, I gave her the form of sharing, the hollow words, the hollow arms, but women know warmth or the lack of it. I mourned the boy in a private place.*

Helm pressed his advantage. "You heard Purji on her worshipers and what they needed. The urge is no different in us. To lose that lonely, vague and vulnerable self in an Absolute. Yeshua admits his belief and goes on waiting. So will I, but how will you defeat me when you argue from an abstraction and I from a primal human need?"

"Yes, it's always easier to wallow than to think," Speed said. "Thought was too hard won for me to be traded for an uncritical prayer, much as I'd like to have prayed and known I was heard. I don't know if mine was a lack of faith or merely a more precise definition, the idea of perfectible Man against the Absolute of God. Hardly new."

"Hardly." Helm shivered in a cold he had no body to feel, shoulders hunched against the emptiness around him. "Shall we to business? There's no comfort in chaos."

Speed's cruel streak couldn't resist the jab. "You prefer the illusion of order? Look there!" Deep in space an alien sun flared nova. "Someone else's cosmology going up in smoke. Just a matter of time for us."

To Peter Helm, such lights were not those by which souls were illuminated; he held to his point. "Don't put Candor on the stand. Sum your case without him."

"You serious?" Speed peered at the little lawyer. "By gum you are. Worried, too. He's already an embarrassment to what you're selling."

Helm shrugged. "So he is, and so I might have predicted he would be." That much of human history never changed. Catalysts were useful at the inception of a great cause but a hindrance later. The trial was never about Candor anymore than World War I was fought over a Serbian assassination or the Civil War over John Brown, yet the fool and his overt, futile act were always needed.

"Give me one good reason why I shouldn't gut him like a hog in November."

"A trade," Helm offered. Speed knew the game and used the fool deftly to his own ends. "So that I need not inform the determined lady from Lexington. You disappoint me, Speed. Was a mere wife such a burden?"

"I never knew much about women," Speed admitted. "Less about love. I only felt it once, early. After that, love was always safer at a distance."

Helm allowed tactfully that women were difficult at best. "I can understand the distance, but why total anonymity?"

"Why yours?"

"My work is obviously not done. But you," Helm wondered. "You were an idol, an icon, one of your country's greatest—"

"Butchers," Speed finished the thought, biting down hard on the word. "I became what I most despised: the Robespierre girded with noble motives and squeamish at the blood I spilled." *Merely ambitious at the start. Not a zealot, not even a statesman at first but drawn deeper and deeper into a sink of principle that couldn't be denied, terrible as it was.*

"Yes." Helm's tone softened with an unusual empathy. "I turned away sometimes from the rack and the stake, wondering where the engine I set in motion would stop. But even when I urged clemency, my followers broke or burned them anyway and screamed for more."

"Speak of catalysts," Speed mused. "I walked among vindictive, jealous men convinced they should have my place when they could barely fill their own. Blind, ruinous men whom I wanted to boot out the door and tell them: all right, you do it if you think you're a better man. But the responsibility was mine. Just that I was wrong so often stumbling toward an ultimate right and the number of the dead mounting while the vindictive men said they told me so . . . and I wrote the orders that meant more death. Why should Hitler have such a bestial image when I was the father of modern warfare? Anonymity? I'd be anything, the Void itself, rather than identify with that."

Helm felt the first sickness of attenuation, yet Speed was drifting away from Earth toward black nothing. "What do the deaths matter? I've burned men for holy principle and would again. The principle is all that matters, the end."

"There's the difference," Speed noted out of a deeper sickness. "I never slept well enough not to hear those numbers tolling in my sleep."

"We're going out too far!" Helm warned. "I can't think clearly out here. Why oppose me, then? Sum your case—a fair secular case, I admit. What's Candor to you but an absurdity? Why put him on the stand?"

"That self-serving son of a bitch makes me want to take a bath."

"He's an American like yourself."

"The definition's paled."

"An American for today," Helm persisted. "Look at your country today. Impoverished in spirit, waking from the illusion of individual sovereignty to that of God. There never was a people since time began who so needed to be in the right or a time when right was so hard to find. Are they not sick to death of moral ambiguity? You speak of numbers; consider these. Over twenty-three million functional illiterates who can't read a newspaper, let alone the phrase 'moral ambiguity.' They see their country torn between crippling secularity and the law of God. Crying for God, why shouldn't they see the Reconstructionists as right? The Constitution won't save your country, Speed. Wherein does it sustain them? Only a new order of Christianity can do that. A hard choice, true, but one they're desperate enough to make."

"Checked only by an inconvenient Constitution."

"I said a hard choice. Faith in God is not democratic, that's a given and always has been. What is more blasphemous or absurd than a referendum on God's will? Look!"

Helm pointed down to Earth. "You and I can spin here in limbo speaking of irony and dichotomy. For most of them down there, that democracy was only a cruel joke that gave them nothing where faith at least gave hope. Even if Yeshua told the truth, just a confused carpenter drunk with an idea of God, what will you give *them* for the void left by his absence? Choice? The responsibility of utter freedom? You've wrestled with that terror as I have. You said you'd rather be part of the Void."

"Why not?" Speed said firmly. "If it's a desert, at least no lie can live out here."

"Yes, it's pure," Helm lashed back. "Pure and chill. One can hear those vast cathedral spaces between the lines of harmony. You're worse than secular, you're naive. Humans crave absolutes and will have them, now more than ever. Tell them there are none and what will you offer instead? Adams, Jefferson? Lawyers' reasons? English reasons by English theoreticians once removed, pursuing their passion for freedom while denying it to others on moral grounds. That won't work, man. It never has. If you think it will now, you're a bigger fool than Candor."

Josh Speed only laughed, did a tight turn and bank, shooting toward Topside. Helm shouted after him. "If you put him on the stand, I'll reveal you, I swear it!"

The answer came back faint with distance. "They were calling me fool back in Pigeon Creek. Come on, it's already tomorrow."

Helm's energy recharged as they neared Earth. He accelerated and overtook Speed. "Why are you so obstinate against God's will?"

"Not against God's will, but yours, Helm. People like you can never kneel to the Cross without your foot on someone's neck."

"The minute he takes the stand," Helm promised, "Joshua Speed ends. You'll be a monument again, not a moment's precious solitude."

For some time there was no sound except the faint rushing of thin atmosphere as they skimmed over Earth toward Topside. Speed spoke at last.

"You and I should hang out a shingle together. Two bastards back to back. Who could beat us?"

15

Now it's time to play "You Bet Your Life"

In the press box, Nancy Noncommit murmured clipped instructions into her headset. "Camera three, you're my floater. Letti Candor's up in Section C, first row. Find her. If they put Candor on the stand, be ready to give me close-ups. Blood, tears and sweat, okay? Everybody stay sharp. Got a lucky feeling today." She gave Cathy Cataton her bland on-camera look. *Lucky and mean.*

Aurelius entered. The court and spectators rose, then settled down except for Joshua Speed, who stepped away from the Plaintiff's table, removing his antiquated spectacles.

"Please the court, I call Lance Candor to the stand."

What Noncommit called lucky feeling, Cathy Cataton knew as a gut instinct for news about to break. "One and two split: Speed and Candor. Three float on my cue."

The cameras focused on Lance Candor renewed their love affair with that marvelously photogenic young face, the boyish forelock nervously pushed back only to flop forward again, the open American expression as incapable of guile as Lance was of spelling the word.

Now the hero shared screen with Speed as he beamed at the witness, homely as a bucket. The freshet of applause grew steadily into a torrent as Letti bounced up in Section C.

"You tell 'em, honey!"

Joshua Speed waited obligingly through the applause and whistling. When he spoke to Lance, his manner was courteous and friendly. "I admit myself at some disadvantage when my witness comes to the stand as honored in death as he was in life. You're from Kansas?"

"Neosho Falls," Lance stated proudly. "The heart of America."

An obligatory spattering of cheers from the Kansas contingent. The Senator from Wisconsin appeared at Helm's elbow. "Okay, he did it. You want to pull the plug on Speed?"

"Yes," said Helm. "Advise the lady of his alias and present location." He kept his eyes on Lance and the affable, clumsy lawyer, who would have looked more at home behind a plow. One of them was a dangerous idiot, but it wasn't Speed. The man was calling his threat with no thought of the consequence. Not without finer instincts of his own, Helm knew Speed was as committed as himself, but not the why of it. How could the man be so intractable in the face of Divine will? *I could have hanged or imprisoned him in Geneva.* Helm sorely missed the Swiss efficiency and damned the inconvenience of democracy.

"An honorable life," Speed repeated for the jury. "An eagle scout, active in your church and community. Not to mention the heroism that led you to sacrifice your life for the President's. No greater honor could redound to an American."

Lance stood straighter in the box. "As an American I would ask for none."

"As an American. How old were you at the time of your death?"

"Thirty-one."

"Honorable and brief. Married?"

"Letti and I got married right after high school."

Speed's lopsided grin warmed with nostalgia. "They did that in my time too. Nice to know some folks hang on to the old ways. You died in Washington; would you refresh me on the business that took you there?"

"A religious mission. A delegation of Christian Reconstructionists."

"Reconstructionists." Speed tasted the word. "That would imply rebuilding something."

"Rebuilding America," Lance replied vigorously. "From the heart out. You see, we believe—"

At the Defense table, Helm lowered his eyes in disgust.

"—in the absolute authority of God and Scripture."

"Indeed? Over what?"

"Over everything."

"Including civil law?"

"Everything."

"Well, that's a lot of ground to plow." Speed pulled at his ear. "I only regret God can't be called as a material witness to that mandate. What was your specific aim on this mission?"

"We went there to plead for God in government. To put God back into our laws and schools."

Speed whistled softly. "You folks don't do anything small, do you? I take it from that statement you don't believe in separation of church and state."

There could be no separation, Lance insisted. There were only two states of meaning or value, that of Grace and that without it.

But was he not mindful of the Constitution?

"What Constitution?" Lance quipped. "Where have you been, Mr. Speed? It's been said again and again, the Constitution won't save America."

"I've heard the sentiment." Speed paced away from the witness box. He turned back, hands clasped behind him, knees slightly bent, head raised like a farmer sniffing for rain on the wind. Most observers were concentrated on Lance. Few noticed the new tone in Speed's line of questioning; just a little sharper. "I own to some confusion. Do you mean that ultimately democracy cannot save the United States?"

"Law is clear," said Lance. "And sometimes truth is hard. You can't vote on God. There are the saved and the unsaved. We knew that when we went to Washington."

"Excuse me, sir. By 'saved' you refer to a state of Grace?"

"I do."

"In which happy state I trust you shuffled off the mortal coil."

For a moment the wry allusion was lost on Lance. "Yes. I hope you did too."

Speed shrugged. "Can't say. I was murdered. As my favorite author put it, sent to my atonement my crimes as flush as May."

"Sorry to hear that, sir."

"Don't see why." Speed's razor neatly decapitated the sentiment.

"The murderer viewed me as you viewed Coyul, incarnate evil to be removed by violence. The same fanatical contempt for the law."

"Objection!" Helm rose. "Is Counsel questioning the witness or giving a sermon?"

"Sustained. Counsel will frame questions the witness can answer."

"Allowing that you're not an expert witness"—Speed's eye flicked back to Helm as he thought to head off further objection—"how does this state of Grace work? How does one know if he's in this blessed condition?"

"Well, by communion with the church and through Christ. By visible signs in life."

"What signs?"

"Well, God favors with true communion and prosperity those he has chosen as his Elect in Heaven."

"Through Christ," Speed mused. "You were present yesterday when Yeshua of Nazareth testified. How did you regard that testimony?"

Helm was on his feet again. "Object. No matter how cunningly Counsel phrases the question, witness is called to render opinion on a point that would confound a qualified theologian."

"Sustained."

"As a layman," Speed qualified, "you said that prosperity on Earth is one of the visible signs of God's favor. Then the dirt-poor don't have much show at all, do they?"

"Well, I'm not an expert," Lance said, "but you have to be saved."

Speed's features wrinkled with incomprehension. "Have to be chosen and saved. No matter how virtuous or selfless: Mother Teresa in India, Father Damien the leper, Father Ritter saving kids from the streets in New York, thousands of all faiths and convictions, who lived and died with no credentials save faith translated to serving others? No chance at all unless they're saved? Mr. Candor, this is the old argument of Grace against good works."

"Sir?"

"Look it up. His Honor might refresh you."

"Yes, Augustine." Aurelius nodded. "After my time, but adamant on the point."

"I won't ask you to testify as an expert, Mr. Candor, only if you sincerely believe in this severe definition of salvation."

"Yes, sir," Lance answered stoutly. "I have believed it all my life. And I'll go further. I'll say this—"

Helm sued silently to a just God for patience, hoping for another legitimate objection before this incredible ass hanged himself with no help from Speed.

"I'll tell you this: whatever I've done, I don't interpret God's law, only follow it. To see that law reign supreme in America or here, I'd rewrite any damned constitution you can name!"

A classic moment for the cameras. Lance was media manna, valiant in close-up amid a torrent of cheers and applause from the audience. Speed waited it out. "Would you, sir?" he countered mildly. "All for God's will?"

"I would."

"A will that regulates a predestined judgment?"

"Well, that's the heart of it," Lance asserted. "It is predestined."

"Sheep and goats already culled? No freedom of choice?"

"God's will has never changed. I've only followed it."

"Which implies an exercise of choice," Speed observed.

"To use the sense God gave me," Lance riposted with the look of a tennis champion returning a wicked serve low over the net.

Speed smiled affably. "Let's assume you're right. God's will has never changed."

"That's not assumption but truth, sir."

"Well, I'm a little confused." On monitor screens the lanky lawyer looked anything but confused. "If you had followed God's will in the fourteenth century, you would have howled for Wyclif's blood because Latin was the holy language and he had the audacity to translate Scripture into English. Following that will in the sixteenth, you would have either burned Protestants for their heresy or Catholics for their obstinate orthodoxy. Or cited that same orthodoxy to oppose Martin Luther when he stood on individual conscience. In the eighteenth you'd have opposed those very safeguards that allowed you freedom of conviction. In short, every enlightened advance since the Dark Ages. Human rights. The right to say no. Not interpreting, Mr. Candor? With a smug assumption of God's will you descended on Washington to supplant the very document that gave you the right to hold such conviction."

"Object!"

"You were free-translating the hell out of God's will when you threw that bomb at Coyul."

"Your Honor, Defense objects!"

"Then how will it be in your reconstructed God-fearing America or

Topside when someone turns you down flat and says no? 'No, I'll follow *my* conscience, not yours.' "

"OBJECT!" Helm shot out of his chair. "Counsel is baiting the witness, who never said he was an expert on theology or the inconsistencies of American history."

"Denied. Question is inference from direct testimony," Aurelius quashed him. "Defendant's actions are assumed to stem from his convictions."

"They do," Lance yelped. "I'm not a liar. What has the Constitution allowed but confusion and injustice? America is falling apart while they argue the Constitution—"

"Interpreting again."

"There's *got* to be one authority nobody can question!" Lance shouted. "What else could that be but God and the Bible?"

"Witness will restrain himself," Aurelius cautioned sternly. "And Counsel will frame answerable questions, as I have reminded him earlier."

"I will, Your Honor," Speed promised. "Let's take a look at this proposed new order of things," he began on a new, easier tack. "No doubt to be swept into power on a tide of enthusiasm, a power based solely on God's will with Scripture as the inerrant writ of that will for those people you call the saved. Life is not gonna be a hayride for them. Since it replaces Constitutional law, this Divine Will would have to cover every facet of everyday life. Is that correct?"

"Yes," Lance agreed. "Yes it would. It does."

"Even to a man's business, his dealings in the marketplace?"

"Of course." Lance felt more confident on firmer ground. "The Bible deals with fair weights and measures, even authorizes gold as a standard of value."

"I see." Speed paused, jingling change in his pocket. "Then I take it that my house and life would be exposed to this inerrant writ."

"Especially your house, Mr. Speed."

More appreciative laughter from the house.

"Which means you extinguish the right to privacy, making legal judgment on the most personal matters. A grave responsibility." Speed produced an old-fashioned pocket watch and wound it reflectively as he moved toward the bench. "Please the court, and to spare my colleague further objection to sermonizing, I would like to place on record certain historical results of such a theocracy; then, on that basis, pose simple and quite answerable questions to the witness."

"Court has no objection provided there is substantiation. Defense?"

Helm sighed. "No objection with that proviso. I would be glad to see my learned colleague surrender the pulpit for the law at last."

"My intention, sir." Through the patter of laughter, Speed managed to look chastened and modest. "I submit that what Mr. Candor suggests and represents is exactly what such a theocracy accomplished in Massachusetts with stocks for the smallest infraction and gallows for alleged witches. This is fact. This is precisely what some followers of Bhagwan Shree Rajneesh did in Oregon less than a decade ago with as ruinous result. This is fact. Even more recently, Oral Roberts solicited millions from his flock on the alarming assertion that God was going to cancel Roberts' lease on life and call him to premature Glory unless the faithful forked over a given amount by a certain date."

Speed squeezed the bridge of his nose between thumb and forefinger. "Not the absurdity or even the bald audacity that makes one gasp, but the millions that were straightway sent in response. Apparently God relented; Mr. Roberts is still with us, but perhaps my colleague is right and I should take up the cloth. You can't argue with the salary, and you don't have to convince a sensible jury of your motives. In my time, Your Honor, men like that sold snake oil remedies from a wagon."

"And in mine," Aurelius recalled drily. "If man's first gift was fire, the second was fraud."

"I put it to you, Mr. Candor, that this is spiritual fascism. The more total the trust, the more dishonorable the fraud. Is this what you support?"

"Well." Lance swallowed, running nervous fingers through his hair. "I don't know about that Bag-somebody or Massachusetts or whatever, but what are you asking of me? I said truth is hard. Very hard, even . . . even for me sometimes. But if God's will is absolute, someone's got to speak for it."

"And again I cite another precedent for your case. In the 1960s, there was a case of an American husband and wife charged with sodomy in their own bedroom, accused by their own daughter—one puzzles over the method of detection—and prosecuted under an existing law of the state of Illinois. In the twentieth century, that legal instrument was still on the books. Do you stand for a law that can breach your privacy and hang your personal life on the public washline?" Speed turned away.

His hands described incomprehension in the air. "Is this what you believe?"

"I don't know anything about that either." Lance hesitated, aware of erstwhile firm ground sinking under him. "But I guess—"

"You guess? You stated! No facet of life exempt from this relentless moral scrutiny."

"It—has to be that way."

"No idea, no book or work of art, no simple urge, isn't that true? I refer to your earlier testimony. Did you not work for such a reconstructed theocracy that should and would remove the fundamental rights of privacy you enjoyed in Kansas and still enjoy here? No private place exempt from that inexorable consistory of your neighbors? No hope of salvation but through the house brand of a faith enforced by prison or death? Is this not the true picture of what you endorse?"

Lance looked like a man forced to pay out money he didn't have. "I have described what I believe, sir."

Speed now stood in the center of the court area, facing the audience and cameras. "If this is a true picture of your beliefs, how in hell can you call yourself an American?"

Lance bristled. "I *am* an American. No one can believe anything else. I died as an American. I know . . . I know it seems that one belief doesn't go along with the other, but it does. It can. I'm an American, all right, Mr. Speed. I wouldn't be anything else."

"Then I've only one more question for you, son." Speed moved in close to the witness box. "This inerrant authority you invite into your house and your very bedroom: how will it deal with you and Ms. Ginsberg?"

I knew I felt lucky. Noncommit ordered, "Close on Candor. Tight!"

The monitor close-up revealed a face too white for color TV, absorbing the full shock of the damning question. Lance's mouth worked; a sheen of perspiration covered his cheeks. Following her own instincts, Cathy Cataton punched up a quick shot of random audience stunned into utter silence, then split between Candor and Letti, whose kewpie-doll face was a study in trauma. Her fingers fretted at her sprayed hair. She stammered something to the large woman next to her. Cataton mourned that Letti wasn't miked—

"—he saying? That dirty-mouth man? Why's he say a thing like that?"

"Never you mind, Letti," Bernice comforted her. "He's just trash, you know that."

"Lying about mah husband." Letti quivered with a feral rage. "Goddam shitass *liar.*"

On either side of stricken Letti, friends fluttered and whispered with offered tissues and feminine judgment, not all for publication. "Well, I never . . . do you think he . . . well, I'm her best friend, but you know Letti always had trouble with that."

Letti moaned, "Oh mah God oh mah God." Her reddening gaze zeroed in on her husband. In that lowering scrutiny one could read dark memories and something darker gathering like a Gulf storm.

For the benefit of primetime coverage, Joshua Speed asked helpfully, "Shall I repeat the question, Mr. Candor?"

—as Lance sent a furtive but urgent SOS to Helm and Scheherazade Ginsberg rose out of her seat with a wrath as biblical as Letti's but quicker to act.

"Shall I?"

"Mr. Speed," Lance choked, "you are no gentleman."

Speed's smile remained sanguine. "Not today."

As Speed, the audience and the merciless cameras watched, Lance Candor began to weep.

Helm sprang to his feet ready to fight. "Objection. Again he's baiting the witness with a wholly unsupported, irrelevant and immaterial allegation."

Scheherazade heaved and writhed her way clear to the aisle, a tigress to the defense of what she held dear—

"A cheap grandstanding trick with nothing to substantiate—"

"LANCE!"

Thousands of heads craned around at the apparition in paisley jeans and cerise hair streaking down the aisle toward Lance Candor.

"Get her," Cataton snapped. "Never mind the fish on the stand."

—as Scheherazade plunged past Speed to clutch Lance's hand. "Tell him to go fuck himself. There's nothing irrelevant about us. Remember what we stand for."

Lance could only gape at her.

"Honey, what's to be afraid of? We're dead anyway. Remember what you did for the President. Remember me on the reactor. Remember the Weathermen. We *stood* for something."

—as Noncommit fairly drooled over a split image of Lance's cheeks blossoming perspiration and Letti gasping like a beached fish, one hand to her Chaneled bosom, and Cataton implored her faithful Benny, "Can you get that broad on Candor's mike?"

"All I get is his heavy breathing."

"Shit." In one Olympic leap, Cathy Cataton swept up her portable recorder; in another she was out of the press box heading for the nearest aisle with Nancy Noncommit no more than a second behind and trailing imperatives in her wake: "Stay on the whoziz with the hair. Cataton is not gonna scoop me."

She overtook Cataton in a few strides and hauled her up short, all girlish concern. "For God's sake, Cathy, get a Tampax. You're *starting.*" In the split second necessary for Cataton to realize she couldn't be, her Below Stairs counterpart was past her with a three-length lead, sprinting down the aisle and fifty yards across the Megachurch in 4.3 flat, a gold medal time. Twelve seconds out of the starting gate, with Cataton a full length behind, Nancy Noncommit thrust her mike in Scheherazade's face. "Say it to BSTV and the world, honey. Are you having an affair with Lance Candor?"

"Sure I am," Scheherazade crowed, grabbing the mike in one hand, Lance's palsied paw in the other. "Lance will never deny me. I won't deny him."

Lance looked faint.

"But it's not just an affair. This is love," the heroine of nuclear resistance affirmed for the cosmos. "I mean we are *dedicated.*" Scheherazade felt a sharp tug; she appeared to be clutching a disembodied forearm, five of Lance's fingers, palm, coat sleeve. The rest of him had slid from view down into the witness box in a profound faint.

A new sound rose from the audience, a rising, manic roar of laughter and released tension. Somewhere in the rear a fight broke out and showed no sign of pacification. Letti Candor was being forcibly restrained by friends. Aurelius rapped harder, but no one heeded him. Helm sat rigid, surveying Speed with the gloom of a pool player doomed to a corner shot from behind the eight ball.

"Mr. Candor?" Cataton and Noncommit strained far over into the witness box, down into its shadowed depths, microphones dipped like buckets in a well. "Would you like to make a statement?"

Watching it all on television, George Kaufman snapped imperious fingers at Ricky Remsleep. "Fetus, come here. Look at this."

Ricky only glanced at the tube, busy with his guitar. "Yeah, that's Ginsberg. She always has the hots for revolutionaries."

"Kid, read my fingers." For the first time in life or death, Kaufman got physical. He grabbed Ricky by the shoulder and hauled him in front of the tube. "Not her, birdbrain. Take a look at a good second act curtain." Kaufman's cynical eyes glowed with the memory of opening night hits and failures. "Correction, a *great* one."

Cameras found dream coverage wherever they focused. Lance ashen and oblivious in the depths of the witness box. Letti, unmiked but scatological, crying to be loosed to murder. Cataton and Noncommit warring for *lebensraum* around Scheherazade Ginsberg, symbol of liberation. Aurelius pounding his gavel in a fruitless demand for order. From nowhere, the face of a sallow young man thrust into the very eye of a BSTV camera, waving enthusiastically—

"Hey, Brain! Here I am, see me? Are we square?"

—and Josh Speed, tranquil in the storm's eye, hands in his pockets, grin broad as the prairie that spawned him. His sorrowful face, too burdened with care to be lightened by just any joke, now glowed with the brilliant light of classic absurdity. His grin widened and broke in a horselaugh that gave every indication of running as long as a Kaufman show. He clumped over to Helm, shoulders still heaving.

"Your witness, sir."

■ 16 ■

Double-parked in the City of God

"Candor, stop that!"

Peter Helm ranged the antechamber off the arena, trying to marshall his formidable thought processes. Trying to make Lance concentrate, difficult since the tarnished White Knight had retreated to escape mode and kept re-running his funeral in Wichita. When Helm looked at his client, he was as liable to see a flag-draped casket as the unhappy young man whose case he now had to pull out of the fire. Not a gambler, Helm still found them useful as weathervanes. From 3–1 odds in his favor, handicappers were now quoting 7–5 against.

Again he saw the casket, rattled by the newest volley of shots fired over Lance's grave. *"Stop* that."

Reluctantly Lance tuned out past glories and gave his attention to Helm. The treacherous Speed had shattered him, and Sherry was just too much at the wrong time, love her as he did. But the reporters came; the trial was about him again. Throughout the proceedings and the arguments he could barely understand, he'd begun to feel irrelevant to the whole business and nagging doubts about his own motives, all made clearer through living with Sherry. Now that he wasn't horny all the time, his mind worked in ways he once would have called backsliding.

Speed's line of attack brought home one indisputable fact of omission: he had never considered for one moment that what he strove for to save America was against its deepest principles. He could always pronounce his religious aims and the Pledge of Allegiance in consecutive breaths. Not that Speed had changed his mind, just it was something to think about and maybe talk over with Sherry. Was it that he believed so strongly to begin with or that belief made him feel like part of something that appeared to be moving? That question took considerable mental gymnastics, but for the first time in his life or death, the mind of Lance Candor asked him just what he did believe and stood there with arms folded, waiting for an answer.

But they laughed at him. People like himself. That hurt. What kind of people would laugh at a man who gave his life for the President? Just because his wife didn't like sex and forced him to look somewhere else. Well, if the cat was out of the bag, at least the cat stood up for him.

Staring up at furious Helm, Lance didn't care how mad the little bastard got or much about what happened now. Whatever Helm or Speed or even Letti thought, that was tough darts. Something had snapped. There was a phrase he'd read somewhere, something about personal priorities. Lance was now groping these neglected considerations into some kind of order.

"I knew what Speed would do to you on the stand. Now I've got to repair the damage you've done. I told you. I gave you clear orders not to see that woman again."

"I know, Mr. Helm. Except you didn't say why."

"Didn't—Candor, can't you hear me?"

"I mean you never asked why I might want to see her."

Helm stopped pacing. He was once and might be again a supreme spiritual leader, not used to explaining orders. The fuzzy, dreamlike quality in Candor's voice annoyed him but rang no warning bells. "You are not important in this."

"I know."

"You were never important except as an image on which we displayed an issue. Painful as that may be."

"No. Not anymore."

"Good. When I put you on the stand, answer exactly as questioned and no more. Volunteer nothing, do you understand? How long has this been going on?"

"How long has what been going on?"

"Candor, you strain belief."

"Well, try harder!" Lance shot back with a new aggressiveness that surprised both of them.

"That—description fails me—that motley-hued companion of yours."

"What's it matter? You said I wasn't important anymore."

"I must be prepared for any attack on you."

Lance got up, straightening his tie. To Helm's amazement, he simply brushed the question aside. "I'll handle that, Mr. Helm. What are you going to ask me?"

"Quite simply if you admit your guilt and repent of it."

Lance's expression, an erstwhile open book to his lawyer, was now opaque. "Oh."

"Are you ready?" Helm opened the door. "Do you hear them out there? I must put them back on your side. Do you think that is easy? Yes, you do: they're your kind of people, howling along with you after Coyul. But remember an interesting habit of wolves, Candor. If the quarry wounds one of them, they stop to tear that unfortunate apart. Call them believers or what you will, they are a pack, a mob I must sway, and they are far less interested in your gossamer motives than your adulterous bed."

"I'm learning that." Lance peered closely at the little lawyer. "Who are you, anyway?"

"How should you know me when you can't even recognize Joshua Speed?" Helm ventured a slight smile in which one might sense centuries. "I'm on your side."

"I wonder. What side is that?"

"Come."

"No, wait. Don't tell me what to say out there."

"Candor, I am losing patience—"

"I mean it. No matter what he said, I'm an American and I have rights."

"Do you?" Helm challenged delicately. "You waived those rights gladly when you proclaimed the law of God superseded the Constitution *in toto*. Which it does. God is not a democrat. You can't have it both ways. Come along, Mr. Candor—and if you must admit feet of clay, try to keep them out of your mouth."

Lance was nervous waiting to take the stand, jiggling loose coins in one hand. He scanned the audience to find Sherry. They'd have a lot to talk about tonight. At least he could talk to her. As for Letti, she still hadn't come to see him and he guessed she wasn't about to now. Tough darts, he decided, liking the go-to-hell phrase and the heady new sense of liberation. His gaze drifted across the court space to Speed, whose head was bowed over his notes. The gaunt head came up suddenly. Something in the profile plucked a chord of memory in Lance. He rattled the coins and considered Helm's instructions. Then—

The coins.

"Mr. Helm."

"Don't tell me. You cannot need to go to the lavatory."

"No."

Helm went on writing in his minute hand. "What, then?"

"Nothing." Lance contemplated the face on the coin in his palm. The stamped profile was idealized, majestic as that fuller image he'd once revered as he'd read the words on the flanking marble panels. Lance stared at the coin, then thoughtfully returned it to a pocket as Helm rose to address the court.

"Your Honor, Defense desires only cross-examination of the Defendant before summation."

"I see. Plaintiff?"

"Plaintiff has no more witnesses to produce."

"Defense may proceed."

"I recall Lance Candor to the stand."

No one applauded this time as Lance took his place on the stand. The jury looked bleak and the acres of people around him seemed to send a very different message to Lance now. Out of the vast, rustling sibilance he heard smothered sniggers and boos. When he thought about it—and today Lance was thinking with unaccustomed clarity—that seemed unjust. They cheered him yesterday. Before they laughed. He recalled Helm's admonition on the social habits of wolves and his eyes went again and again to the homely giant seated next to Coyul.

Helm's normally cool manner was now warm and solicitous. "Mr. Candor, after the emotional bullying inflicted on you yesterday, I will be as brief as possible. I hope you were not too distressed by my colleague's tactics, and I can only hope for the remainder of this trial that he will not resort to them again. I daresay every Christian spirit in this church is with you; how could they not be when everything you did or said was from convictions shared by them? Mr. Speed would introduce secular confusion into consideration of God. A faith that relies on fallible thought incorporates doubt, and I am sure you had none."

"Your Honor." Speed elevated his lanky frame from the chair. "I was under the impression my colleague wished to cross-examine, not summarize."

"I too," Aurelius said. "Which will do much to explain why I so strongly lean toward hearing that summation in the Void. Defense will cease oration and return to his stated purpose, that of cross-examination."

Helm stood corrected most graciously, and addressed his remarks directly to Lance. "Did your actions throughout stem from your religious beliefs?"

The answer was barely audible. "Yes."

"Do you still believe in the sanctity of your purpose?"

Lance's hesitation was apparent. "Yes." He shifted restlessly in the witness box, eyes always drawn to Speed, surer than ever now. The *yes* felt wrong somehow. He didn't know what he truly believed anymore, not with such a man against him.

You can't have it both ways.

"You were given no chance to explain yesterday. Do you deny the allegation raised by my colleague regarding the woman known as Scheherazade Ginsberg?"

"I—no. I don't deny it."

"Thank you." Helm turned slightly to face the jury. "A simple, manly admission of guilt. In all the years of your marriage, was this your only adultery?"

"Adultery?" On television, Lance looked as if he were backing away from the word. "This . . . this was the only one."

"The only one. Remembering God's forgiveness and your hopes as one of His Elect, do you sincerely repent?"

Nancy Noncommit admired the image on her monitor: Lance struggling with conflicting emotions on unfamiliar terrain. "I don't feel sorry for the little S.O.B., but Helm's a bigger one." Then her practiced eye caught a totally alien nuance in Candor that suffused the boyishness. He looked directly at Helm.

"I feel dirty."

"Of course you do. And you repent of this woman?"

"I feel like I got sold."

Helm shot him a look of veiled venom. "Please answer the question as put to you. Do you repent?"

"Why?" Lance burst out suddenly, full of anguish. Helm took a moment to realize the *why* was not an insolence to him but a plea to Joshua Speed. "Why, sir? Why did you do this to me?"

"The witness will answer the question!" Helm demanded.

Lance ignored him, eyes riveted to Speed. "You were my hero. I can't understand why you're against me. What have I done?"

"Mr. Helm is examining," Speed reminded him. "I can't answer while you're his witness."

"Witness will answer," Aurelius ruled, then added an afterthought. "Unless he chooses not to where answer might be prejudicial to his case. Refresh me, Mr. Speed. Does not your Constitution include such an amendment?"

"It does, Your Honor," Speed responded from his chair with an encouraging smile for Lance. "Number five."

"That's right," Lance remembered. "The Fifth Amendment. No. I decline to answer under my rights—and I would like to be excused."

"Call the Hilton, leave a message," Cataton ordered Benny. "I want an interview with Candor." She remembered the ploy Nancy used to get at Ginsberg first, and that time was ripe to do unto others.

Below, Peter Helm exhibited his meager equivalent of apoplexy, a slight but definite reddening about ten-to-two eyebrows. "You little viper"—under his breath at Lance—"you utter turncoat, what are you doing?"

"I'd like to be excused," Lance requested of the court with dignity. To Helm, with more determination than the lawyer would have guessed in him: "I don't know just what it is I do repent, sir."

"*What?*"

"I mean, didn't you say this was the House of God? If it is, I can pray here and I can find answers, and I sure as green apples can be confused here without God minding or the roof coming down. I am confused, and I wish you'd let me go home."

■ 17 ■

Christian reconstruction

CANDOR TAKES FIFTH!
FLAT END TO HIGH DRAMATICS
IN CANDOR TRIAL

"I'm Cathy Cataton for Topside News, here's what's happening. Trial judge Marcus Aurelius ordered a change of venue for summations in the Candor trial, saying: 'I'm tired of the circus and so is the jury.' Summations will be heard in the Void. Lance Candor, whose relationship with Scheherazade Ginsberg was dramatically revealed by Ms. Ginsberg herself yesterday, has not rejoined his wife but is still in residence—some say in hiding—at the Hilton Hereafter . . ."

"Candor!" Helm snapped like a distempered dog at the phone in his hand. "What in hell do you mean you've agreed to a press conference? The trial's not done just because they're not hunting your skin anymore. Your skin and any other facet of your negligible existence are the least of what is at stake here."

Helm listened with scant patience to the usually indecisive voice at the other end into which a new and growing stubbornness had crept. Candor was *not* seeing the light.

"Candor, listen to me. Until this trial is done, you'll be seen with no woman but your wife." Helm had met Letti and knew what he asked. "You will not see that Ginsberg woman, not even by telephone, do you understand? Candor? Do you hear me . . . ?"

Lance heard him. Lance made answer. Helm lowered the phone to its cradle, stunned by the advent of a turned worm.

"He told me to go *what* myself?"

JUDAS TO COYUL, URGENT: MRS. SPEED DEPARTED FOR TOPSIDE. DELAYED AS LONG AS WE COULD. INFORM SPEED. ADVISE.

COYUL TO JUDAS: GO AFTER HER, JAKE. SEND SOMEONE TO SLOW HER UP. TAKE HER SHOPPING WASHINGTON. SHE NEVER COULD RESIST A SALE AT GARFINKEL'S.

The decoy should be handsome, courtly and outrageously charismatic. For one hasty moment, Coyul thought of Wilksey Booth—but no.

COYUL TO JUDAS: COULD YESHUA GIVE HER A VISION IN LAFAYETTE PARK?

JUDAS TO COYUL: YESHUA DOESN'T DO VISIONS AND SHAME ON YOU, BUT JACK BARRYMORE INTERESTED. WOULD LOVE TO APPEAR AS JESUS.

Coyul relaxed a little at the godsend of Barrymore. No one distrusted women more than Jack, but none could charm them more thoroughly.

COYUL TO JUDAS: PERFECT. SHE'LL LOVE HIM. OWE YOU ONE. ALL BEST XXX

Coyul painfully missed life Below Stairs, where he only had to stage-manage mad actors, jaundiced critics, fascists, romantic pagans and those penitents who insisted on suffering, at least until the novelty wore off. Post life there was so easy and sane . . .

Meanwhile, the star of destiny once more, Lance Candor was discovering that heroes dated as quickly as magazines. His hotel room awash with reporters and cameras, the questions barraged him too rapidly for reply, none about his religious convictions. They were far more interested in his glittering present than his pristine past.

"You said you felt dirty. You mean about Ginsberg?"

"How long have you been living together?"

"When will Miss Ginsberg get here?"

"It's Ms.," Lance struggled. "She thinks Miss is sexist."

"Do you plan to get a divorce?"

"Is your wife divorcing you?"

"Have you read *The Hero's Lady?*"

"You plan to write the story of your own life?"

Lance hadn't and didn't, but the notion attracted.

"How do you feel about your wife's book?"

"Well, honestly," Lance floundered, "I'm trying to find out just how I feel."

"Does Scheherazade plan to write her own life story?"

"Which life?" Scheherazade blazed from the corridor into the center of the room and all attention. "We're too busy living this one."

"Sherry!" Lance waved desperately like a sinking swimmer sighting rescue. "Am I glad to see you! Where've you been?"

"Sorry, lover." Scheherazade took his arm as predatory cameras surrounded them. "Went out to check my computer horoscope and got hung up at the head shop."

Flashbulbs popped, microphones prodded them. Scheherazade wrapped herself around Lance in a photogenic clinch.

"Hold it. Give us another? Great."

"Are we ready?" Cataton checked her people. "Ready remote? Just let the tape roll, Benny, we're going for *vérité*. Okay . . . we're live."

Live and exclusive, Cataton reflected with the satisfaction of malice. She had leaked a phony rumor to BSTV that Candor would be at home this morning, reconciling with Letti.

"Right on." Scheherazade flopped into an easy chair, crossing her legs. The view was startling given the brevity of her skirt and dislike of underwear. She lit a joint—"Anyone want a toke?"—and passed it to an appreciative reporter.

"What are your plans?" Cataton pressed her. "Will you and Lance marry?"

"You never know with a Scorpio." Scheherazade traded the joint to Cataton for a filtered Camel, firing it from a kitchen match struck on her low-heeled shoe. Lance was shocked.

"Sherry, what's this? You don't smoke. Cigarettes are carcinogenic."

"What ain't, lover?" She dragged deep and favored Cathy Cataton with the purposeful appraisal David might have reserved for Bathsheba.

"I'm indicated for a major change, like the Wolf Man in full moon. A whole new phase."

"Move in closer, Lance. Lean over her in the chair."

Lance dutifully bent over his lady. "Well, look, I wanted to say something about the trial—"

"Will you write your life story?" Cataton plied Scheherazade.

"I've always wanted to. Even got a great title. *Life on the Firing Range.*"

"I think that's firing line. Terrific. Is it real love between you and Lance?"

"To the max!" the scarlet woman informed the cameras.

"How do you feel about public reaction to your relationship with a married man?"

"Hey, man, we're not responsible for their hangups." The cigarette between Scheherazade's teeth bobbed with every syllable. "Lance and I respect each other. Like, we didn't have oral sex until the second night."

Letti saw it all on a closed-circuit monitor in the Hilton lobby.

In the cool atrium, fountains splashed and sparkled, ferns waved gently in an *ersatz* breeze, and an ethereal young woman played Chopin on the lobby grand. The Hilton was not where Letti usually gathered with her ladies, but today she hoped she might accidentally encounter Lance amid the psychological security of her friends. He would be embarrassed, Letti wounded but a lady as always, and she would allow him home to "see" about their differences.

She and her friends drank tea and lamented the abrupt drop in Letti's book sales and the cancellation of her Ever After commercial. Letti drank cup after cup, but no sign of Lance and none of the other ladies showed any inclination beyond tea. Should she order a cocktail, hoping they'd follow suit? No. She wouldn't give them the pleasure of seeing her take the first, they'd talk behind her back.

Letti suffered. Then, salt in all the wounds, *he* was there on the lobby TV monitor. In Letti's hearing, Chopin drowned in a growing thunder of war drums. No breeze cooled the flush of shame from her cheek. She saw—and her friends saw—that harlot Jezebel who grabbed Lance by his nasty old *thang* and led him off by it. Letti believed in marriage if not in sex. Why should he go off with that little tramp when she had made him the nicest home on their block and the only one with matched porcelain dogs by the fireplace?

With growing wrath, she observed that the brazen hussy didn't have any underwear, bad as that woman who lived with the Devil. Now Lance put his arms around the Unclean and kissed her—

"Oh my land!" Bernice gasped. "She's puttin' her old tongue in his mouth. Right on *tee*vee."

"LAY-ANCE!"

Not murder in Letti's eye but judgment. She rocketed toward the nearest elevator with her loyal Bacchantes close behind just as Nancy Noncommit impacted on the outer lobby revolving doors with a crew behind her.

Closed-circuit monitors recorded the ladies' interlude in the elevator, dialogue jumbled but eloquent; saw them eject from the car in full cry, Letti in the lead and her pack baying her on. She reached Lance's door like a storm front. The door was open, saving her the brief delay of breaking it down. Her maddened glare fell on her husband in full embrace with the Woman of Gomorrah. The cordon of reporters and cameramen were no deterrent to the flying wedge of outraged decency. Lance barely had time to identify the doom descending on him like a dive bomber.

"Letti. For God's sake—"

Until now, Letti's passage had been closed-circuit only. Now she was live on TSTV and, a moment later, on BSTV as Nancy Noncommit reached the room bare seconds behind her. To a delighted post-life audience, the hero's lady telecast her most enduring comment on a love to last beyond death.

"YOU LI'L SHITASS!"

She raked her formidable nails down Lance's face and kneed him accurately in the balls. Lance crumpled while Cataton glowed at the *vérité* of it all. She didn't even mind that Noncommit had made the show in time.

"Grab a view, Nancy."

The cameras feasted on a classic visual repast. While Letti's large and robust friend Bernice fell on Scheherazade and shared in her dismemberment, Letti kicked and clawed at the fallen Lance. More impassioned than systematic, she began with his face as he writhed on the floor. Spittle flying from her lips, she juicily gouged out his eyes and broke his jaw.

"DIRTY, NASTY—"

Working downward, she called on two friends who could find no working space on Scheherazade, to assist in breaking and detaching Lance's arms. He shrieked at each violent subtraction. "Letti, you're killing me—"

"Wish I could, you—"

Armless, soon to be legless, Lance could only moan as thirty nails ripped through his skin and abdominal wall as if rummaging a deep carton, sure that what they desired would be at the bottom.

"SUNVABETCH!"

"Get this," Noncommit purred to her cameramen. "Get the blood."

"Beautiful," Benny chortled to Cataton. "And this new tape, you don't have to worry about light."

Lance resembled the Scarecrow of Oz after the number done on him by the flying monkeys. "Letti," he croaked feebly, "I've raised my consciousness. Can we talk about this?"

"SHIT."

Unravaged area on Lance was now difficult to find. One helpful matron battered his teeth out with the base of a heavy lamp. When Lance's shattered ribs punctured a lung, a geyser of blood rose, spectacular as Old Faithful under the furious pounding of Letti Candor. A nearsighted woman commenced his decapitation with her nail clippers. Slow-going and not effective on bone, a problem solved by smashing the vertebrae with the lamp base and then wrenching in concerted effort until Lance's head came loose.

They swarmed over the two culprits like ants over dropped picnic food until, at last, apparently nothing remained unbroken or in its original place. Then Letti's red-lit eye fell on the root of her suffering: that nasty white worm he was always trying to stick in her. Her claws came down in the manner of an earth shovel, bit in and ripped.

Vengeance.

Letti wiped her red hands on the rug because there was blood enough on Lance's nice shirt and so hard to wash out. Mania dimmed; she became aware of the cameras.

"Bernice, gimme my hat, please."

She set the chapeau at her usual prim angle, recovered and donned her white gloves as she spoke for posterity. "All I can say is my mommy and daddy would never stand for this. My dirty—"

Letti faltered, quivering. She meant to say "daddy." What had escaped her, though Freudian as hell, was hardly a slip. With a Comanche yell of restimulated mayhem, Letti hurled herself again upon the residue of her husband. There must be *something* left to break.

"YOU HAW-MONGER!"

"Now, Letti," Bernice interjected a ladylike note of restraint, "don't get yourself upset, You'll spoil your makeup."

Cataton stubbed her Camel in an ashtray. "Let's blow, Benny. Don't bother to edit. We'll run it all again on the six o'clock."

"Sure," Nancy Noncommit suggested. "Right after the Latter Day Saints family togetherness spot. Thanks for the bum steer, sweets."

"Do thou unto me, thou shalt be done twice," said Cataton with a demure smile.

"I've covered hard news all my life," Nancy challenged. "Who'd you fuck to get here?"

"Nobody, dear. I was a nun. They wasted me in Central America. I was as politically inconvenient as that poor fish on the floor." Cataton blew her rival a kiss and sailed out the door. "Look it up."

"Hell, let's wrap," Nancy decided. "And watch the gear. Those two are still spraying blood."

The fourth estate and Letti's entourage departed, leaving the carnage for the maid to clean up. They left behind the hollow, tremulous silence that follows a hurricane. The severed head of Scheherazade Ginsberg opened its remaining eye. Lance was not in her limited field of vision.

"Lance? Don't worry," she encouraged out of the ruin of her larynx. "To be revolutionary is to suffer."

Somewhere someone mumbled wetly.

"What, baby?"

Lance found enunciation difficult with no teeth. "I don' know 'bout you, but I'm 'ginning to get pissed off."

Coyul and Purji sympathized with the experience of their eons over the violence they'd viewed in large-screen color. They agreed to skip the six o'clock news recap.

"Poor children," Purji sighed, "they're bound to be disoriented. They'll be days getting it all together again. Took me hours myself."

A surprise to Coyul; she hadn't mentioned being dismembered by the Keljians.

"And very rude they were, too," Purji recalled darkly. "They're still ages away from anything like sense or mercy."

"They certainly could use a Jesus. Shorten the process."

"Meanwhile." Purji dissolved from the couch and reappeared at the salon door. "Shall we, dear? The babies need changing."

Monsieur Canard, manager of the Hilton Hereafter, was all fluttering hands and Gallic apology while his pessimistic concierge Marcel could only gape at the red devastation left in Letti's fearsome wake.

"Vitement, Marcel." A snap of M. Canard's manicured fingers. "Remove the leftovers. Prince, Madame, one is appalled. We can assure you this has never, *mais jamais,* happened before, nor will it again. Marcel, the entire cleaning staff."

"No, no. *Pas de tout,"* Coyul insisted. "We will not trouble your staff. Madame and I would rather manage by ourselves. *Merci bien."*

The management apologized yet again for the breech of decorum, and one could expect better security in the future. A squad of young Jesuits, perhaps, or former Vatican guards, preferably body builders. M. Canard and the concierge bowed out of the ruined chamber.

Purji winced at the carnage. There was blood everywhere, on the Ché Guevara poster and the one in pastels declaring WAR IS NOT HEALTHY FOR CHILDREN OR OTHER LIVING THINGS. The furniture was sodden and the floor unspeakable.

"Like a jigsaw puzzle in a hurricane," Purji mewed. "Where on earth do we start?"

"You take Ms. Ginsberg. I will attempt the martyred Lance."

Purji lifted the head of Scheherazade. "Can you hear me, child? I know this is traumatic but it happens more often than you'd think."

"Just . . . get me straight," the head husked bloodily.

Purji's apprehensions were well founded. Even in post life, carbon-based humans were difficult to reassemble. Ego and libido were involved. Flesh-locked imagination tended to fantasy. Under the guiding hand of Coyul, Lance labored, groggy but game.

"Here we go. A place for everything and everything in its place. Lance? Lance, you're not getting the hang of this at all. Concentrate."

Lance tried. Reassembled only from the chest up, he convulsed through a steely-eyed approximation of Clint Eastwood but with Cyrano's proboscis.

"Keep trying, boy. Purji? Do you have a rather large lower colon over there?"

"Just putting it in. Difficult to fit."

"Shouldn't wonder, it's his. This is hers."

"Thanks. I can't find her appendix anywhere."

"Check for a scar. Maybe she had it out."

"So she did. You are a treasure, darling."

Even with the essentials restored, Lance didn't look right to Coyul. He squished and rattled with every movement. Ego had dictated the lapse into Eastwood. Now pure burgeoning libido seized his loins. Never hugely endowed and still in shock, Lance awarded himself a penis out of legend.

"Now, now. Eyes bigger than our stomachs."

"I like it," Lance rasped. "How'm I doing?"

"Epic, my boy, but in view of human limitations, shouldn't we downscale a bit?"

On second thought, Lance modified the impractical organ to something fine but realistic.

"Feeling our old self?" Coyul inquired.

"Reborn," Lance managed hollowly. "Through suffering."

Letti's assault had not diminished his inexhaustible flair for self-dramatization. The erstwhile hero rose on one elbow like a child's toy incorrectly assembled, blinking at Coyul. Whether the difference in him resulted from maladjustment or trauma, Lance's mien was definitely changed. "That . . . damn, I can't even talk."

"Thought so. Open up. Say ah."

"Ug . . ."

"Yes, I certainly did," Coyul clucked over him. "Purji, we have the teeth mixed up."

She brightened, a problem solved. *That's* why she looks so paleolithic. Need your teeth back, angel. Sorry about that."

There was another glitch, a small damp object that should go somewhere in Scheherazade but Purji hadn't a clue. "What is this? Never saw one before."

Coyul squinted at the unlovely bit of viscera. "Oh, it's her gall bladder. Throw it away; she'll never miss it."

"That's not tidy."

"So be a purist. Put it in."

Scheherazade floated upward to total awareness, gratefully sensing a whole body again where anything below the neck had been conspicuous by absence. As with Lance, ego and libido cut a disruptive swath through Purji's efforts to help. Her breasts blossomed to pure Monroe beneath a rugged but incongruous resemblance to Rock Hudson. Beyond her fog, the sexiest voice in creation was encouraging gently. Her own nature responded with radically altered signals.

"Try for consistency, child."

That was the problem of a mercurial lifetime. Changes were coming. Scheherazade had felt their onset for days. Her eyes, fluttering open, were rewarded with sight of the most ravishing creature fate would ever set within human reach. Like Lance, she was reborn, but with an arresting difference. She felt healthy, aggressive and horny. Gazing up at that peach-and-honey vision, Ms. Ginsberg salivated.

"Sherry . . . ?"

Somewhere close by she heard the voice calling, but destiny pulsed in Scheherazade like fevered blood in her ears, drowning out all but that ineffable siren-voice and that smiling, luscious mouth she longed to kiss.

"You are the most." She stroked Purji's flawless cheek. "I would love to lunch on your boobs."

Purji had a moment of uncertainty. "Did I get everything in the right place?"

"Perfecto, baby."

"I didn't forget something?"

Wolf Girl whispered huskily, "Let's go somewhere and check it out."

■ 18 ■

The treacherous Wycherley

No court, no solid appurtenance of the law, no spectators. Only the star-scattered dark Void and eleven human figures shadowed or sun-silvered as they drifted two thousand miles above Earth. The group kept their approximate court positions, six jurors in one group, Coyul and Speed to one side, Helm to the other, all facing Aurelius and the clerk.

To Speed, the jury looked uncomfortable. Few were equal to the loneliness and isolation that bore down on humans in space. The first to be truly fit for it were being bred in this century, and who could say how their descendants would imagine infinity when light-distant wonders became common?

"Here no plebes will disrupt consideration," Aurelius began. "No cameras will translate clean thought to false image. Here in this silence, a thought is heard like a plucked note in a still room. The court has considered how often human truth is drowned in human need or fear.

Let us then give as much consideration to that purity as to music. Counsels and jury present, we may proceed with summation. Mr. Speed?"

As that awkward scarecrow floated out to face the jury, Coyul found it amazing that none of the Americans on that panel had yet recognized him, but why should they? They were used to the statues and his sonorous words dulled to platitude in the mouths of gaseous politicians. The original voice was unimpressive, the man himself a disappointment to myth-seekers. Only the eyes held to the legend, the look of a man grown up facing west to endless forest when the heart alone put limits to freedom. He first saw men in chains in New Orleans and carried the scar of that sight for a lifetime along with a definition of liberty as deeply etched.

"Ladies and gentlemen," Speed addressed the jury. "This has been a civil trial for damages based on the Defendant's assumption that my client's identity was other than as testified. Coyul is not the Devil but what he represents, an alien charged with developing our potential to its fullest. You've heard his testimony and Purji's in corroboration of his origins. You've heard Yeshua of Narareth, and finally the Defendant himself in what we must assume is an accurate representation of the beliefs of his church. I need hardly remark that the issues at stake overshadow both Plaintiff and Defendant in their magnitude. Let me then deal with those issues.

"My colleague speaks for one side of that question which has confronted men for thousands of years: the need for absolutes in a world that keeps changing. He offers as a solution to contradictory mandates a rigid totality of belief. Expedients, like healing drugs, must be administered with care. The moment you resort to morphine against great pain, you begin a chain of dependency that grows and strengthens with each repeated dose. Mr. Helm will tell you that the end justifies the means. Absolute power as a means to a benevolent end. No. As with the pain killer, we cannot come unaddicted from the abuse. We can say as much for history. We cannot escape or ignore it.

"Two sides of an irreducible argument are put before you. Can Man live by rationale alone? Not without hungering for an Infinite, a God he can conceive but not encompass. What men can imagine, they will carve. Can he live by faith alone? Not without throwing blinders over his common sense and leading it like a frightened horse through the fire of reality, a threat in every ray of light that pierces the cover.

"We are left with a disparity, the price Man pays for his humanity, that he can look up at the stars around us and feel small in one breath and in the next wonder what is beyond them. The ideal versus the actual. The political realities of a free people in a working but flawed democracy, versus the absolute of God's law. That which must change versus that which is immutable. We must live with this enduring disparity. To deny one side for the other is to deny half of our nature. To destroy either for the sake of the other is spiritual suicide for both, the free faith and the free mind.

"This is the kernel, the core of what you have heard and must weigh. If my colleague is right, then every secular doubt or objection that enters your mind is a deviation from and a danger to the stasis of God's law, punishable by the secular arm. If he's right, then there are nothing but absolutes, and we who wonder, question or deny are alien. Our very powers of reason become at worst evil and at best insanity, an imbalance that threatens perfection.

"If you find for the Plaintiff, you live and believe as you will—imperfect, incomplete, untidy, inconsistent and illogical as that life and faith may be. If you find for the Defendant, tomorrow someone like my learned colleague will be telling you what to believe or risk trial yourself.

"Well—it's been said, perhaps in the course of this trial, certainly in America within the last few years, that 'democracy is the great love of the cowards and failures in life.' I don't know how that goes down with you, but it sticks in my craw. When the fat's boiled down to soap, I'm giving you a choice. Mr. Helm is telling you to buy him or else."

I suppose Barion and I didn't do too badly at all, Coyul thought as Speed relinquished the jury to Peter Helm. *Trouble is, like pure radium in pitch blend, for every Josh Speed, you get thousands of Helms and billions of Candors.*

He took his lawyer's hand, very much wanting to hail him by his rightful name. "Josh, if I were a constitutional monarch instead of an appointee, I'd make you a knight. But you'd probably argue with that, too."

"Don't polish your dubbing sword," Speed cautioned, eyeing Helm. "We ain't out of the woods yet. How'd the jury feel to you?"

"Master Wycherley seemed pensive, but he's read that way all along. The stockbroker is bored, more curious about the Dow Jones closing index than your arguments. The Lutheran suspects Helm, both women hate your guts, but at least the Catholic stayed awake."

True, they were still deep in the wildwood.

"This is indeed a civil trial," Helm began before the jury. "Had it been criminal, my client might have been able to put before you a clearer picture of his motives. As it is, the Devil as Plaintiff chose a case which allowed him to cloud the contention with irrelevant testimony. Such as his alleged alien identity, corroborated by whom? Another alleged alien. To which he added testimony by someone who alleged himself as Christ. The meat of this testimony alone would constitute a separate trial for evaluation and strain the wisdom of theologians, let alone the six honest lay persons of a civil jury. In this ploy, one perceives more tactic than truth.

"My client did not perjure himself on the stand. I need not hammer on this point. You were witness. He defined his beliefs in direct examination and reaffirmed them in cross, beliefs which some of you and a majority of the court spectators continue to hold sacred. He declined to answer only in regard to an essentially irrelevant issue, his mistress. We can conclude nothing about Mr. Candor from this—or the unruly interruption of the woman in question—but that he committed a sin of the flesh, regrettable but not central to this case. We can conclude a great deal more about the moral timbre of my colleague in raising the issue to confuse your judgment.

"As Mr. Speed chose to do, let me address the deeper ramifications of this trial. If you are honest with yourself, you cannot choose between convenient parts of two opposed philosophies and call them the considered product of your conscience. There is no melding point between fallible human authority and the clear mandate of God. Then ask: how much of human error has stemmed from attempts at such an adulteration and palpable compromise? Set the immutable law of God as laid down in Scripture against human precepts bent and twisted every day to suit secular purposes. You cannot shop for moral right as between competitive goods in a common market.

"I have wondered in the course of this trial on the question of right and challenged even my own conclusions. Question the inerrancy of God's law in Scripture and it fails of reason. What is conclusive in that? Deny the founding logic of any assumption and it falls. These are intellectual games and evasions invented by the fallible mind of Man, a creature in whose inherent nobility Mr. Speed misplaces so much faith.

"Question the law of God—and find that through all the translations, that word remains constant. Question the law of God, divide between Caesar's due and that of God, and find that one makes the other impossible. Question the will of God and you find that nothing can exist outside that will, not even evil can exert one finger without that will. Question as you will and find that your life and actions have been based either on a mountain of vague questions or one clear answer.

"If you are all, as you profess, faithful Christians, quite obviously this Topside is not the end, not Heaven but a limbo known even to the pagans. A way station on our journey to judgment, neither good nor bad, neither edged with suffering nor gilt with reward. Does that prove that these ultimates do not exist? Grant a doubt there, then in what condition will you arrive at that final disposition of your own case?

"Find for the Plaintiff, by whatever name he calls himself, and you must conclude that what you have believed all your life and even now is only a relative truth. A shifting, temporary expedient as so much else of human belief. Find for him and you choose the vague question in which the very lack of clarity affords a cowardly comfort and evasion.

"Find for the Defendant and you reaffirm that belief in the eternal which has sustained you. That witness who called himself Jesus said himself on the stand: not the fact of his identity but the faith in it that shaped our beliefs and our survival as a people.

"Whatever his failings as a man, Lance Candor acted from that faith. How stands your own, and what will you do for it?"

Helm floated away from the jury to resume his place.

"I commend both counsels for clear presentation of their arguments," Aurelius said, "and for refraining from those earlier tactics which necessitated this change of venue."

He gave final instructions to the jury regarding their latitude of verdict. They might find for either side or in any degree between Plaintiff and Defendant or rest evenly divided, needing only a majority to one side or the other. Aurelius directed them to deliberate at some distance from the court. None of them could return Topside for any reason until a verdict had been reached.

The jury trailed off after Wycherley until they were small in the distance.

"Now we wait," said Speed. "The machine is in motion and can't be stopped. I wouldn't have it any other way. He would." Meaning Helm, alone and apart from the court, turned outward to the Void, his whole stance one of defiance.

"He hates it out here," Coyul remarked, "but he won't give in. As much of a gadfly to his time as you were to yours."

"You know him then?"

"I know him. Finally."

"Who?" Speed asked eagerly. "I'd like to know myself."

"He has his reasons for being Helm as you have for being Josh Speed. I must respect them. But he's found you out."

"And informed my wife," Speed nodded gloomily. "Wonder he didn't make it public."

That would have been bad trial strategy, Coyul explained. People saw surfaces and labels. To name Speed would have been to run him up on a flagpole, unmistakable as the stars and stripes. Helm would have divided or lost entirely the American sympathy he strove for. By the same token, his own foreign origins would win no support from American Christians notable for chauvinism.

"So he restricted blackmail to your wife," Coyul concluded. "She's on her way Topside. Will you want to see her?"

Speed considered at length before replying. "No, not yet. Sometime perhaps."

The jury, though distant, was animated by disagreement, gesticulating at each other in eloquent pantomime. "Good sign," Speed diagnosed. "Too quick would be bad news for us."

Coyul didn't quite agree. Out of a job meant out of an impossible dilemma. He and Purji could go where they liked. Nothing grandiose, not even gods but ordinary beings in a quiet place where at last he could begin his cycle of symphonies. Given her leaning toward compassionate deity, Purji might work part-time as a forest sprite, say, prayed to by woodcutters and lost children. Not too shabby as futures went . . .

He came out of his reverie at Speed's light touch on his shoulder. "They're coming back."

"That was quick."

"Quick enough," Speed worried. "And here comes Helm. I hope he doesn't gloat as well as he argues."

Peter Helm braked his momentum a short way from Coyul and Speed. Noting the return of the jury, Aurelius drew in closer from his private meditation.

"Members of the jury, can you return a true verdict?"

Matthew Wycherley detached himself from the others and took a position midway between them and Marcus Aurelius. "My lord, we have a verdict. How true and satisfactory, we leave to the court."

"Verdict is your office, Master Wycherley. Please elucidate."

"We are divided and must render division as a verdict. Jury finds in part for the Defendant. No damages to the Plaintiff. We find in part for the Plaintiff, in that the question of his identity and purposes, despite testimony and argument on either side, is insufficiently proven."

"Insuff—" Helm leaped in. "I move for mistrial!"

"This is, I admit, an ambiguous verdict," said Aurelius. "Foreman will enlarge on these findings before the court entertains the motion for mistrial."

Matthew Wycherley glanced back at his co-jurors, a look that incorporated their disagreement and mutual frustration throughout the trial. "The verdict did stand three to two for the Defendant. I myself cast the vote of balance. Save for myself, this jury is American and of this time. Yet they cannot deny they bring to judgment their forebearers' several beliefs."

Coyul could discern a mixed attitude toward Wycherley in the jurors' demeanor alone. Only the stockbroker and the Italian stonemason seemed content; the rest were plainly unhappy.

"Thus did I bring my own belief and custom of law insofar as this court allows. In the north of England and in Scotland, a verdict of insufficient proof was valid to conclude and dismiss a case. According to my conscience, I could not weigh with the majority. No damages to Plaintiff, no measure against Defendant."

"This is a mockery of justice," Helm interjected sharply.

"More a quandary," Aurelius vouchsafed. "Master Wycherley, an evenly divided verdict can be final in a civil case. Such a verdict in a case like this—I may now speak of it—where the Plaintiff's authority is at stake, throws open the door to challenge and further trial of the religious issues. A motion has been made for retrial. Have you anything to add before I rule on that motion?"

"Yes, Your Honor. I urge the court to consider our verdict just beyond any question of mistrial. There was, in my time, much letting of blood over faith, and much injustice. As much in other countries, true, but with us there was something . . ."

Wycherley paused, choosing his images from the heart, words to describe the wordless root of instinct. "Other countries like France and

Spain saw this bloodletting as a necessity of faith; in England it was seen as unjust and dangerous to men. We were ringed with enemies, Catholic and Protestant alike—"

"Not without reason," Helm reminded him venomously.

"—and the rights we had won of our nobles were too hard come by, one by one. These others of this modern time never knew such a struggle. I could never forget. Counsel for Plaintiff said that we must live with the disparity between the laws of God and those of men; that above all other arguments did persuade my conscience. Those who conceived Master Speed's constitution knew in their blood as well as their minds that these laws are and must remain separate, even a contradiction. They cannot clash without ill use to both or damage to men—and I am much amazed that an English ancient must repeat this lesson to those of a country bred from my blood and bone. If the American Defendant had known by what painful travail his civil laws came to exist, he would not so lightly have set them aside.

"Upon mine honor this is a true verdict. Heeding the law and trusting in God, the jury begs to be discharged."

Master Wycherley bowed his head to Aurelius and rejoined the jury. There was silence as Marcus Aurelius regarded the Englishman. Helm broke the hiatus.

"A devout Englishman is a contradiction in terms, Master Wycherley. France would have preferred England's belated altruism to the butchery my grandfather saw. Your Honor, on the basis of this shoddy verdict, Defense moves again for mistrial."

"Motion denied," the court ruled. "You will have to flay the issues in a separate case. Verdict being rendered, the jury is discharged and this court stands adjourned *sine die*. Master Wycherley, please conduct the jury home to Topside."

"I suppose I needn't pack after all," Coyul observed with no enthusiasm as the jury dwindled in the distance. "Thank you, Josh."

Marcus Aurelius joined them, no longer magisterial, waving Helm to make a fourth. "Neither of you is the most immaculate of counsels, but passionate you are."

"And remain," Helm said doggedly. "I will appeal. I cannot accept this verdict."

"In light of the verdict, that right is implied," Aurelius reminded him. "As for Master Wycherley—"

"Whom God must surely despise."

"Or at least ponder," Aurelius modified. "Even in my time the folk of that island were beyond comprehension, possibly as a result of their endless fogs. Coyul, I would imagine Mr. Speed has not so much saved you for our future as sentenced you to it."

"Imperator, you put it irreducibly."

"Then I'll summon my clerk and be gone. Peace, gentlemen." Aurelius' invocation was as much suggestion as blessing. "Hail and farewell."

Aurelius left them.

"I suppose you're to be congratulated," Helm said to Speed. "As our Roman colleague said: incomprehensible. You were seven eighths of sublimity, Speed."

"I've let a great deal slip during this trial and must get back to it," Coyul told them, "but may I offer you both a drink first?"

"Thank you, no." Helm moved away from them, not toward Topside but out again to the Void. "There will be another time and another case."

"In which, if possible, I'd like you both on my side," Coyul called after him. "Well, I still have a job, Josh. Unfortunately, dealing with your lady goes with it. Coming?"

Like Helm, Speed was turned to the Void and the stars. "Tell her . . ."

"Yes?"

"Nothing. I supposed I loved her, but I always needed to define what I meant by love. I should just have put my arms around her. On the other hand, she was never quiet enough to invite the urge."

"I heard most of your speeches from Cooper Union until the end," Coyul said. "You never took an easy road to anything."

"After Cooper Union, there weren't any. Go along, Coyul. I'll stay here for now."

"The Void again? Even I can't take this for too long."

"There's company of a kind." Speed pointed out toward Peter Helm tensed to withstand a bald universe of mud, rock and fire his senses could not deny but his soul must. "He has to conquer this, Coyul. He has to make it care about him." The rangy lawyer swiped a huge paw across his face to hide discomfort. "What'll you say to my wife?"

"God knows." Coyul never sold himself short on charm, but the lady from Lexington frankly daunted him.

"What a coward I was," Speed said suddenly. "I was never in love with her. That has nothing to do with a good marriage. She was a good wife. How much pain I gave the woman by not wanting to hurt her. That was an easy road I've regretted. Goodbye, Coyul."

What else Joshua Speed thought was, as ever, lost in the shadows of that complex, private mind. He was already moving away toward the Void, gaining momentum to overtake his cosmic opposite. Coyul had wanted to offer both a place on his staff. As of now a legal staff would be a good idea. From the indications, he'd need all the good lawyers he could find.

Coyul let himself drift Topside slowly, in no hurry to resume the duties of a pro tem deity. He was tempted to give them what they wanted, a Hollywood kind of God. More of them envisioned H. B. Warner or Max von Sydow as Christ than would ever buy Yeshua. For himself, he lacked the ego and vindictiveness for any conventional god or demon. For job satisfaction or sense of accomplishment, forget it. The pay wasn't worth the grief, except now and then for a Speed or a Wycherley.

As for Speed's wife with her historically short fuse and imperious nature, perhaps Queen Victoria might take her up socially. He'd speak to Gladstone and Disraeli. The ladies could spend decades of afternoons over tea, politely disagreeing and serenely content. Both were opinionated, both had lost much sleep over Joshua Speed and both would have a great deal to say about the hell of dealing with the man.

No worm unturned

In his room at the Hilton, Lance woke alone and wondered where Sherry might have gone. He was hugely gratified to find all of himself. The Devil had done a neat job. He really couldn't go on calling Coyul a devil when he'd helped get him and Sherry together again with nothing asked in return. Besides, when Lance explored his feelings, religious fervor seemed oddly absent. Letti was going to be very surprised when she saw the new Lance. He started to dress, then hesitated at the mirror, nudged by inspiration. Go for broke, the impulse told him. Live.

Lance imagined a dressing gown in rich blue brocaded silk and added a foulard like Coyul's. The effect was dashing.

"I deserve it. This was a trial and a half."

The trial! The verdict must be in. Lance willed the TV on to Cataton's news. He *must* be top story. People wouldn't be talking about anything else for months, maybe years.

". . . was disclosed today as Reverend Arlen Strutley, in a tearful confession to his Topside flock, admitted to 'grievous moral transgressions.' "

Lance switched to BSTV. There he was, all over the rug like an exploded view of machinery, Letti still tearing at him. There was a particularly graphic close-up of his head being wrenched clear of his neck. Lance couldn't feel nausea anymore, but the sensation came close. He switched back to TSTV.

There was a woman talking about Reverend Strutley, whom Letti had always revered. The woman was a very tough-looking type, the kind usually found Below Stairs at the Club Banal or other questionable places Lance had only heard about. She was responding to questions from an off-camera interviewer.

"Yes, I always wanted to write my life story. I only went into the life to support my political candidate. But this john, honest, I didn't know who he was for the longest time. He never wanted to get it on, just weird stuff. Smear me with whip cream and lick it off, stuff like that. Sometimes he threw in fresh fruit."

"Hey, my trial," Lance interrupted. "Where's my trial?"

"What trial?" Nancy Noncommit put her head into shot to peer at Lance. "Oh, your trial, the poor man's Jimmy Stewart. That's yesterday's news. Try Cataton. She's big on rehash."

Lance switched to TSTV and Cathy Cataton.

". . . and that's the morning news roundup. Recapping yesterday's top story, Mrs. Letti Candor had a great deal of comment while dismembering her husband in the Hilton Hereafter, but nothing for broadcast."

Another brief clip of Lance's arm caroming off a wall, and the remains of his face. Lance looked away.

". . . meanwhile the verdict is in on Candor's trial. No score, no hits, runs or errors, definitely a tied game according to the jury. Coyul's government appears in no immediate danger. Despite grumblings from the Fundamentalist coalition, moderate religious sources call the verdict a vote for sanity. You pays your money and you takes your choice. For TSTV, I'm Cathy Cataton."

"Hey wait!"

"Wait what?" The telereporter glared out of the screen at Lance.

"Is that all?"

"What do you want, bugles?"

"What kind of verdict is that?"

"They tied on you, dipstick. No fine, no damages. And the Prince did okay by you, right? Last time I saw you, you were leftover meatloaf. You want neat endings, catch *Bambi.*"

"Aw . . . poop." Lance turned off the set, disgruntled. Like a great movie with the ending cut off. A trial like his, a martyr like him, there ought to be a bang of an ending. Nobody gave a damn.

"Sherry, where are you?" he pleaded to the walls. "What are they doing to us?"

The phone rang. Lance lunged for it. "Sherry? Where did you go? Why aren't you here? Sherry . . . ?"

The brief, chill silence over the line suggested someone other than Sherry.

"Lay-ance? This is your wife."

He was definitely not ready for this. "Oh. Letti. Yes. Uh, what do you want?"

"What do you *mean* what do I want?" Letti screeched loud enough to damage hearing. "I am your *wahf.*"

Lance held the phone away from his ear. "Well, you sure didn't act like it yesterday."

"Well, shoot." A prim snigger. "Y'know me when I get mad. Anyhow I heard how that old Coyul put you together good as new."

"Not quite," said Lance.

Instantly, Letti was all wifely concern. "Oh, Lance, honey, I didn't hurt you for real, did I? I declare sometimes I don't know mah own strength."

"No, but Coyul said"—Lance searched for the Prince's exact phrase —"he said I may have lost something in translation."

"Well, what in hell does that mean?"

"I'm not sure."

"I guess you'll be coming home now."

Boy, where do you get that? Something in Letti's smug assurance triggered a new connection in Lance—or perhaps shunted over something conveniently deleted by Coyul.

"House looks real nice, except I ain't fixed upstairs yet this morning. Lance, you there? Lance, I am talking to you. I want you to come on *home.*"

"I was heading that way," Lance told her.

Basking in the Jacuzzi and at peace with the cosmos, Purji indolently inclined her head at the knock on the open door.

"Good morning, Scheher—ye *gods!*"

Typical of her kind, shock tended to turn her blue before composure rebalanced. Purji went dark blue at the vision framed in the bathroom entrance. Small shiverings of static electricity played over the frothing bath.

Scheherazade Ginsberg lounged against the door in stovepipe jeans, biker's cap perched on her close-cropped head, the multi-zippered black leather jacket hung with more chain than Marley's ghost. The filter Camel clenched between her front teeth waggled in macho punctuation when she spoke.

"Hello, gorgeous. Just wanted to thank you personally for getting me together, you know?"

Purji detected a predatory purr in the honeyed tones, a quality she was at a loss to interpret immediately. "Your ensemble, dear: is this another political statement?"

"I mean the moon has changed." Scheherazade advanced on little cats' feet like the fog, with erotic intent. "And here I am, lover: a daughter of Lesbos." Scheherazade ran a purposeful finger through the moisture glistening on Purji's perfect left breast. "Think of us as sisters with fringe benefits."

"Darling, hand me the tow—mmf." Purji was handed the towel with a fringe benefit. Scheherazade pounced, tilting Purji's head back and kissing her in a decidedly intrusive manner. Surprised, Purji lost concentration and lapsed into her native light form. Scheherazade found herself tonguing a sunburst. Purji instantly reformed, all apology and solicitation while the daughter of Lesbos coped with temporary blindness.

"Jesus, take it easy, will you?"

"Oh dear, I am sorry. Just that you surprised me."

"I'm fucking blind!"

"Should have warned you. A hazard of our kind—"

"Well, watch it, okay? I have trouble enough with self-image anyway." The lesbic fingers groped forward in a Grail quest. "Where are you?"

"Here, child. So awfully sorry."

"This does not help my insecurities." Scheherazade knuckled her eyes against a universe of dancing lights. "Don't go butch. That's my part."

"Poor Sherry."

"Think you never got cruised before."

The term was alien to Purji. "Cruised?"

"Made a pass at." The chastened Ginsberg opened her eyes warily:

still a light show, but with discernible shapes beginning to materialize. "There you are."

"Cruised." Purji tasted the word. "Like the coastal waters off an erotic beachhead. English *is* a marvelous language. Nothing like it on Keljia."

"No sisters up there?"

"Perhaps, but they lack your *mise-en-scène*. You look medieval. All that steel."

"I can take it off." The obliging Ms. Ginsberg whipped out of the jacket. Wellington boots and jeans followed. "In the Jacuzzi, what do you say? Sex is fabulous in a hot bath." In fifteen seconds, she was naked as an insult, slithering into the foam, undulating herself against Purji like Rhode Island coming on to Texas in hopes of merger. "I always wanted to make it with a god."

"I know." Purji held the girl tenderly like a child to be burped. "They all do."

"Mm, I love you. Jesus, what boobs."

"Ow! Sherry, are you making love or stampeding cattle?"

"Don't put me down," Scheherazade murmured, salivating between the legendary Keljian mammaries. "Sometimes I get off too quick."

"The way you're made. Creatures of the moment."

"But what a moment."

"Like the male bee," Purji reflected philosophically. "The instant of joy inextricable from that of death. Maeterlinck knew you so well . . ."

For Letti Candor, the bottom had dropped out of recognizable existence. *The Hero's Lady* had vanished from respectable coffee tables as the bison from the plains. In her vestigial fantasies of the fallen Reverend Strutley, he now wore a suggestive leer, the horns of a goat and reminded her of Daddy. Now her wayward husband stood in the doorway, thumbs hooked in the hip pockets of tie-dyed jeans, black sweatshirt white-blazoned SEX HAS NO CALORIES, and didn't even look sorry for what he done.

Letti presented what instinct prompted as appropriate: the constant wife, forgiving but still hurt and aloof. No verity unbetrayed, but Letti would be a lady as always and rise above it.

"Lance, ah want to talk to you."

"Yeah. Well." He brushed in past her. "Talk to me upstairs."

Letti jumped to conclusion as swiftly as to violence. "You're always thinking of that. I ain't talking about sex now."

"Neither am I. You're not even warm." Lance vanished up the stairs.

A more intuitive woman might have heard a warning signal. She followed Lance to his bedroom and hovered in the doorway, worrying at the lacquer on her nails. She wanted him back, of course. Any other resolution defied imagination. She wanted him to repent and suffer a little—no, a lot—for the embarrassment he caused her with that tacky tramp who would have given him AIDS or something back home, and serve him right.

Lance gazed around the room at every overdone item: the unwrinkled coverlet, the comb and brush set in mother-of-pearl, the cufflink box, the cologne bottle in arrangement that defied disorder. The polished oxfords aligned on dress parade. The shirts on hangers precisely three inches apart.

"I don't need any of this," he said.

"Any of what, Lance?"

"This."

"This *what?*"

"This stuff. This place."

"You know what I think," Letti flustered. "I think that tacky old Devil put you together with something left out."

"Yes." Lance nodded in solemn agreement, continuing his inventory of Hell House. "And I'll tell you what he left out, Letti. He left out that baby blue coverlet and the baby pink one on your bed, which I didn't get to visit all that much. And the his-and-hers towels in the bathroom, also in pink and blue—"

"That's how it is," Letti protested out of conviction. "Pink for a girl—"

"I know, I know. Do you know how much I hate pink and blue?"

"You never said."

"I was always saying, Letti. You never listened. As a receiver of information, you had an OUT OF ORDER sign hung on you at birth. And moving right along, he left out that stupid lace canopy over your bed. And the fluffy-soft mats in the bathroom. And the rose-scented air fresheners when we don't even breathe anymore. And guess what? He left out the picture window in the living room that never framed any picture worth looking at. And the genuine full-grain leather hassock that you never let me put my feet on. And that awful painting of the kid with the big eyes and huge tears, like he lived inside an onion. And those goddamned porcelain *mutts* by the fireplace you never let me light—"

Now he profaned parental largesse. Wedding gifts. "Don't you talk mean about those dogs! They cost my mama every green stamp she had!"

"And the furniture I hated—"

"French pervincial!"

"And the designer kitchen you never cooked anything in."

"You know I hate to cook."

"Hate it, my ass. You just hated the way it looked without the dishes washed."

"I wanted things to look nice," Letti flared back at him. She couldn't understand any of this. Next he'd say he didn't believe in Jesus or Reverend Falwell. "Don't you like things to be nice?"

But restraint in Lance was a shattered dam; the torrent burst forth. "And that fold-out refrigerator full of microwave breakfasts." The image was too vivid to be glossed over. "Just before the undertaker got to me, I looked better than a microwave breakfast, but hell, I just ate whatever you put on the plate because I didn't know about holistic foods, and—"

He had to stop again before the most painful truths. Putting them in words, they didn't hurt as much as he expected. "And you never liked me."

"I don't like this awful talk." Letti couldn't understand. He was supposed to come back contrite before she forgave him. "I married you, didn't I?"

"That's not what I meant." Lance started down the stairs. "Admit it, Letti. You never liked me worth a damn."

"Where you going? Lance, it wasn't you. It was all that damn sex nonsense. I just got all turned off sometimes."

"Letti, you were born turned off." He stopped at the foot of the stairs, checked by an insight. "You must really love being dead. Nothing gets dirty."

"You know what the Bible says about sex. And shit, it weren't all that much fun for me anyhow. Can't life just be quiet and nice and neat and—"

They were in the living room now, Lance still cataloging with a reckless finality. "Life is not neat."

"This ain't life," Letti maintained. "This is our Heavenly *re*ward. Or s'posed to be, I don't know."

"Well, we got shortchanged, Letti. Goodbye."

"Where you going now?"

"I don't know." Lance opened the door, feeling he needed a Rhett Butler exit. "Maybe to find God."

"He ain't around here, that's for sure."

"No, He ain't. I guess I'll go back to the hotel for a while."

"Back to that li'l whore?"

"I want to mean something more than the *The Hero's Lady.*"

Gone too far. The holy of holies, ruined as it was. "Don't you say a word about mah beautiful book!"

"Hell, you didn't even write it."

"Ah don't care. It was NICE. It was pretty." Letti sniffled—effectively, she hoped. "You were a hero and I was your wife."

Lance looked up at the ceiling. "Letti, that's what ain't. It ain't even minimum wage."

"Lance, you are mah *husband—"*

The door closed.

Letti raised her voice to the commanding banshee screech that had always worked before. "I don't want to start divorce proceedings on you, you *heah* me?"

She hurled the door open to yell it after him—but there were neighbors out in their yards, and Letti was not going to let them know her private business. Why, everyone would be looking at her in church and talking behind her back. She wouldn't give them the satisfaction.

Letti closed the door and listened to the silence. The first thought was involuntary: *least he won't be messing up the house for a spell.*

Once more she was shamed. By *him.* All right, she never liked him that much after high school, but they were married. When she'd fixed herself up, she was going down to that goddam *ho*tel and by God do more than just complain to Lance Candor.

And even her nice Reverend Strutley. You wouldn't think . . .

Yes, you would. Dirty old sunvabetch.

"Messy." Letti made a microscopic adjustment in the magazine display on her walnut veneer coffee table, rearranged the roses that looked so nice. Her pink ceramic clock on the mantel chimed the half hour, and Letti turned from the mundane to matters of the heart.

"Shit. Upstairs."

The rooms weren't straight, not really. Lance couldn't walk through a room without messing something up, and there was her makeup to do over. After all, someone might come. Damn women like Bernice, they had eyes everywhere and always saw something you missed.

Lance felt liberated and defiant as he rode the elevator up to his room. His image in the mirror-paneled walls invited innovation. He added a cigarette. Pleased by the rakish result, he went all the way with a battered slouch hat and trenchcoat. He saluted the classic image and the early retirement of Letti to grass-widowhood: "So long, shweethaht."

Sherry was still out but the red light flashed on the answering machine. The recorded voice was Sherry's, throaty with a new hormonal brusqueness.

"Hi, buddy, this is Sher. Just dropped back to leave this message. I don't want to fuck up your karma or anything like that." A pause, an audible sigh. "Man, this is heavy." The intonations were all wrong for Sherry, not her song at all. More like Lance's old basketball coach in the locker room.

"But like there's heavy changes in my horoscope, and I've met this really significant woman from another planet. Life has called me to Purji's side. Back soon. Ciao." Click!

"Purji?" Lance stared, mystified, at the answering machine that just delivered a karate chop to his future. "But she's . . . where are you, Sherry? I just broke up with Letti and you're not even here. What d'you mean life has called you to . what?"

"I'm sorry," the machine responded in an authoritative masculine voice. "I record messages. I neither comment nor enlarge."

"Ah, shut up."

"Oh, very good. Abuse a captive device. Do you think I'm having fun?" the machine complained. "A creative artist, acclaimed in the field of science fiction, who lived a legend and died rich? I ask you: is *this* a post life for a genius? Recording the labored locutions of an ambivalent flake like Ginsberg? Rather oblivion." The voice went limp with self-pity. "Were it not better to be a mere memo pad? Degradation . . ."

Lance was intrigued in spite of himself. "You died from sci-fi?"

"The term is SF," the machine corrected archly. "There's a lot of it going around, but no. I died rich from starting a religion."

"Now, that's blasphemy."

"No, Mr. Candor, that's commerce. In science fiction, good bullshit goes for eight cents a word. In theology, you name your own price."

"That's not true."

A verbal shrug. "So how come I died rich? This job is a bad rap, but there are compensations. A perfect disguise until I work my next angle. You know what religion needs?"

Lance sat down, thinking of the whole last month. "How about truth?"

"Oh, ye of little smarts," the machine chided. "The secret is to find what people really want and call it self-awareness. Which means you do what you would anyway but without the lip service of guilt. Did I have angles? I was working on an orthodox diet that kept you slim and one hundred percent cancer-free. We couldn't miss. But hark!"

"Hark what?"

"I am picking up vibrations," the machine informed him. "Leather boots coming this way. Ms. Ginsberg, I presume. Excuse me. I will not intrude." *Beep.*

Scheherazade gusted in, waving casually to Lance as she pulled her backpack out of a closet. "Hi, fella. Get my message?"

"Yes, but I don't understand it." Lance did a double-take at her black leather ambience. "What are you dressed like that for? You look like Marlon Brando."

Scheherazade grabbed clothes out of the dresser. "That's the message."

Lance was totally at sea, still unbalanced by his own crossing of the Rubicon. He wanted to talk about it, wanted Sherry to admire and reassure him. That would be only natural for the woman he loved, but she didn't even look like one now.

"What was this about Purji? What's she got to do with us?"

"Everything. She's very relevant to where I am now."

"Relevant?"

"Lance, I'm in love. I have to follow my star."

"What star?" he struggled to comprehend. "She's a girl."

Her packing didn't miss a beat. "You better believe it."

"*You're* a girl."

"Men know nothing of the feminine mystique. Where's my tantric tapes?"

At least he thought she was a girl—his salvation, his education and pearl of great price. Realization dawned in a bleak light. "You mean you're a dick?"

"A what?"

"A female queer?"

"That's *dyke*, Lance." Scheherazade frowned at him. "It is the term of a chauvinist bigot. Try alternate life-style. I am exploring all my potential as a woman."

He stared at her, miserable. From first class on the flagship of a roseate future, he had become a stowaway set adrift. "Sherry, I'm serious. I left Letti."

"That is a very positive karmic move. That woman, even B.O. would leave her. Hey, I like the trenchcoat."

"I left her for you, Sherry. I'm in love with you."

"Of course you are, baby." She dropped the backpack and came to him. "When I'm hetero, I am a force for good in the pool of life, but you gotta be holistic about this. Life is a turning wheel."

"And you just hung one helluva left without signals. What—what does all this mean?"

"Life has called me to her side," she said simply. "Just as it called me to yours. You don't have to understand fate to accept it."

Grief mixed with adoration. Lance tried to accept the inevitable. "So it's goodbye?"

"Who knows, fella?"

"Just let me see you the way you were . . . before. One last time."

"I can't, buddy." Scheherazade sat down beside him. "It wouldn't be me anymore. But wherever I go, I'll always remember you. I want you to keep the peace signs and the Ché poster."

"Sherry, you're tearing my heart out!"

"I'll be seeing you," she promised, "in all the old familiar places that this heart of mine embraces all day through."

The memory was bittersweet to Lance. "I always loved you when you were lyrical. Our room. The dungeon where we first touched and I knew my heart could sing." He wasn't at all surprised when the violins crept in under their farewell; he had expected them.

"In a small café, the park across the way. The children's carousel—"

"Sherry, I think I'm going to cry."

"The chestnut tree, the wishing well."

"Your beautiful pink hair. The way it always changed color with your moods."

"I'll be seeing you in every lovely summer's day—"

"Playing Mantovani while we made love."

"In everything that's light and gay—"

"The way you hate underwear."

"I'll always think of you that way. I'll find you in the morning sun and when the night is new—"

The strings broke off in a trembling hush.

"And you never used my razor to shave your legs."

"Baby, love is little things like that." Scheherazade kissed him lightly in farewell.

If life called Lance Candor to drama, he would be equal to it. He wiped his eyes and tried a tough grin; a survivor, wounded but resilient. "So long, baby. I'll keep your razor by the tub."

The phone buzzed softly.

"If that's Letti," Lance suggested, "I'm not here."

"If that's her, neither am I." Scheherazade went back to her packing.

Lance expected Letti and a shrill stream of invective at the other end of the phone; he held the instrument at a safe distance. "Hello?"

Rather than the squawk of his wife, the urbane tones were an aural blessing. "Mr. Candor? This is Coyul. Purji and I are in the lobby; thought we'd drop up to see if we put you together correctly. Not the easiest job going, and we don't get much practice."

With a lot on his mind, Lance was late on the uptake. "Uh . . . Prince?"

"Just Coyul, old fellow. No hard feelings about the trial, I hope, but we should look you over."

Lance covered the mouthpiece. "It's Coyul and Purji. They want to come up."

"Purji?" Scheherazade scooted for the bathroom. "Bring her on!"

Immediately there was a polite knock at the door. The visitors had skipped the elevator and simply materialized outside. Scheherazade tore out of the bathroom, slapping her cheeks with Lance's aftershave. "*A vivre*, baby! To live is to know the heart of drama. A marital confrontation!"

"I had one for breakfast."

"So it's my turn." Scheherazade hurled open the door, beaming at Purji. "I knew you'd come."

■ 20 ■

The more things change . . .

"Well." Coyul surveyed his restoration job. "How are we getting on? Everything in the right place?"

"Right on." Scheherazade devoured Purji with her eyes. "Perfecto."

"I'm not so sure." Lance sounded that way.

"Give us half a minute to check you out. Purji, inspect Ms. Ginsberg."

"Please don't flash," Scheherazade implored, covering her eyes. "I still got dots."

"You won't feel a thing," Purji promised. "Here we go."

For a few seconds, Lance and Scheherazade were alone. Lance squirmed with an unscratchable itch. "Sort of tickles."

"Kinky," Scheherazade said in a voice full of wonder. "These are weird but wonderful beings."

The inspectors materialized again, reassured. "Not a corpuscle out of place." Purji patted Scheherazade's butch-cropped head. "Coyul?"

"Clean bill of health, although Lance feels better than he looks. What's the matter?"

"Ask her." Lance collapsed into a chair. "I feel awful. It's not your fault, sir," he added hastily. "I want to apologize for blowing you up."

The gracious Prince waved it away. "Professional hazard. As you've discovered, traumatic but hardly permanent. What's the problem?"

Lance hunched over his knees, a tragic figure. "I left Letti for Scheherazade, and now she's left me for Purji."

"It's planetary changes," Scheherazade defended herself. "Can I help it?"

"That's why the sinister ensemble." Coyul took closer note of her costume. "You look like a satanic biker. Purji, have you been irresponsible?"

"Don't be stodgy, dear. To have a public entails obligation. Had to allow it on Keljia now and then."

"There, you see?" Scheherazade glowed. "We shall overcome. Were there many sisters, baby?"

"It's their Bronze Age. They're all too busy trying to live past thirty-five."

"You of all people," Coyul reproved. "Playing musical bedrooms. Promiscuous."

"Coyul, you're putting a nasty human complexion on the whole thing. Sherry, please try to understand—"

"I do." The ardent Scheherazade tried to embrace her. "The first time I opened my eyes and saw you leaning over me, bells rang and I turned on."

"What can I do?" Purji appealed to Coyul. "Help me, will you?"

"Me?" He folded his arms. "Lie in your own bed, you turncoat."

"But I *didn't.*"

"You did, you made love to me," Scheherazade insisted. "It was to die."

"No, child. You made love to me. You were enjoying yourself so, it didn't seem good manners to interrupt."

"Sherry, not only have you broken my heart," Lance intoned darkly, "you are depraved."

"Nonsense," Purji sniffed. "She's barely proficient."

"I am *too,*" Scheherazade hurled back, stung to the quick. "I am a primal force!"

An arguable point to Coyul, who had seen more attractive buffalo. "Well, how was it, dear? Primal?"

"Oh . . . popcorn without butter."

"Snails without garlic?"

"There you have it: something missing. Sherry, did I get that gall bladder in right?"

"She's ruined," Lance groaned. "The love of my life and she just wants to be my brother."

"What can I tell you?" said Scheherazade, creature of the moment. "Scorpios are unstable."

To Coyul the definition was inadequate. She was a sexual traffic hazard.

"I know fate like I know good grass," the hazard appealed to Purji in tones husky with hormone. "Be any kind of light you want. I'll wear shades."

Lance got up, resigned. "I don't need to see this. Goodbye, Coyul. Thank you for everything."

"Where are you going?"

"I don't know. Out there, like Speed. Out into the dark. That's all there is for me now."

"Marchbanks to the core."

"I do love you, Lance," Scheherazade vowed despite defection, "but a star is to follow."

"Stars change," Purji reminded her. "Consider the age difference alone. There you'll be, the rekindled Flame of Topside and myself the pitiful castoff of your wearied lust."

"Honey, that's then," Scheherazade bleated. "This is now."

"All you have is now," Lance said. "That's all you'll ever have. And when your goddamn sign changes again, where'll you be, Sherry? All alone, that's where."

"Only a large soul could love a goddess or give her up," said Coyul.

"Think how much time we could have." Lance held out his arms, inviting. "Eternity almost. I need you, Sherry. I've been burning bridges all morning. You've always talked about commitment but you haven't even lit a match."

"Oh, hey," she faltered, confused. "I don't know if I can deal with this."

Lance took her hand. "Sure you can, baby. I know you can."

Being a large soul appealed to the drama in Scheherazade. She looked wistfully to Purji, bargaining with her instincts. If she couldn't be near the girl she loved, could she always love the boy she was near? Should she bite the bullet, settle for what she could get? Someday, she hoped, she'd get the whole thing straight; one day when the I Ching came out perfect: pass GO and collect the whole bank.

"You'd have to be awful patient, buddy. Until my sign changes, we'd be like two centers in a basketball game."

"I don't care." Lance reached for her, but Scheherazade hung back, desperately appealing to Purji. "He doesn't understand. I can definitely not make his scene. Hell, I'm even flat-chested. Help me!"

"You ought to manage something in that department," Coyul suggested to Purji. "You put her together."

"And rather well, I thought."

"With the imagination of an artist, darling, but finished work is the hallmark of the pro. Do something."

"All right, then. Hang on, Sherry. Fringe benefits." Purji promptly vanished.

Scheherazade squirmed, feeling very odd. "What's happening? I feel like something in a microwave."

"Purji's tinkering," Coyul told her. "Yes, you look better already."

An understatement; Scheherazade's transformation deserved musical accompaniment. The cropped hair lengthened in luxurious waves and fell, thick and lustrous over her bare, smooth shoulders in the electric pink Lance adored. Black leather sloughed away, replaced by a diaphanous and charmingly inadequate garment that revealed most of a truly admirable bosom and other quantum improvements.

"That's enough," Coyul advised to no effect as Scheherazade continued to blossom. "Purji, *enough.*"

Lance marveled. "Look at her!"

"I can't." Scheherazade shuddered, eyes tight shut. "I'm scared."

"Purji, stop showing off!" Coyul admonished. "This is excessive. Why must you always overdo. I said STOP."

Too late. The process had already trespassed the boundary of miracle. The image was still Lance's Sherry but as heavy cream to powdered skim milk. With the revised Scheherazade as a centerfold, you could print the rest of *Playboy* in Urdu; no one would notice.

The changeling gaped at her own form. "Will you look at this bod? I could get horny for *me*. I could—"

Alas, she could not. The urge strangled at birth as Purji finished rewiring mental circuits and reappeared with a flourish. "*Voilà!* Should have done it when I reassembled you. Sort of a junk-food mentality, but we've got you sorted out now. How do you feel, dear?"

"I . . ." Scheherazade swallowed hard. She felt marvelous and, for the first time in her astrological life, stable as a Virgo. She glowed. The look she bent on Lance Candor was soft, fetching and unambiguous. Pinochiette had become a real girl. Purji had even managed the satiny Keljian skin with its delicate hints of blue.

"The shade is authentic. Absolute catnip to males," Purji guaranteed.

Scheherazade found speech a little difficult at first. "Lance, *look* at me."

"I certainly will."

Purji's hand flew to her lips. She brimmed with inspiration. "Coyul, you'll hate me for this, but I have a simply marvelous idea."

"Stop improving. She's already illegal."

"But darling, it's brilliant. Talk about fate."

"What, what?" Scheherazade breathed, beginning to be ready for anything.

In a nanosecond, Purji had shared her concept with Coyul, who beamed his approval. They circled Scheherazade critically; then Coyul clapped his hands in decision. "Yes, Purji: fresh, exciting, original. Though she's a bit small for the job."

Lance took a death grip on his lady. "She's the right size. For God's sake, don't change anything."

"Not for Keljians," Purji frowned. "But they might think it's part of the miracle. Come here, Sherry." She draped an affectionate arm around the girl's shoulders and kissed her. Scheherazade blushed and wriggled in discomfort.

"Uh, do you mind not kissing me. Can't we just shake hands?"

"How would you like to be a fertility goddess?"

"Oh." The notion took a moment to register, then impacted on Scheherazade like the comet that hit Siberia. "Oh, *wow!*"

Purji winked at Coyul, "She likes it."

"I love it! TOO FUCKING MUCH!"

Coyul offered the apple of Eden. "You're a natural."

"Natural what?" Lance looked from one to the other, confused.

"A goddess, baby," Scheherazade whispered, already lapsing into character. "I was born for it."

"We include transportation," Purji threw in.

"But my moon phases. I mean, what if I change in the middle of something? A bummer."

"Shouldn't be a problem," Purji judged professionally. "Perhaps a relapse now and then, but you can handle fifty percent more of the need than I ever could. No one turned away; and take my word, the traffic on holidays—"

"A love goddess." The candidate quivered with ecstasy and anticipation. "A fucking star. I'll draw more fans than Joplin ever could."

True, but no peach without its pit. Purji felt obligated to point out the downside. She'd have to deal with some very repressive patriarchs along the way. She could expect regular attacks, burnings and crucifixions. There was no job security.

"Sherry, think what you're doing," Lance implored. "So far from home among strangers. I'd never see you."

"It's my star, baby. Should I let the greatest bod in the universe next to Purji's go to waste?"

"Wait. Why should he have to?" Coyul posed in the awed dawning of his own inspiration. "Why not go with her?"

"With her?"

"Of course. It's logical, the last note completing a perfect scale. What did we say, Purji? If only the silly Keljians could develop a messiah early on, how much trouble they'd avoid?"

Her mind synthesized the possibilities in seconds. "Darling, what can I say? It's ground-breaking. Boggling."

"Some are born great." Coyul laid his hand on the new-fated shoulder of Lance Candor. "Some just fall in it. Are you big enough for the job?"

They'd lost Lance at the last turn. "For what, sir?"

"Messiah to the Keljians."

"Oh. Well. Gee. Really, I . . ."

"Think, my boy. No homely myth of the stable, sweet as it was. No humble Galilean beginnings. Just—bang! You're there. Christ come down from the mountain."

"A very good point," Purji chimed in from experience. "First appearances are very important, something with color and fireworks. Like a volcano; they have lots. But they'd be in competition, Coyul."

"Pick, pick, pick. Did I say it was perfect?"

"Hey, gang, I got it," Scheherazade leaped in. "Dig this. They think we're in competition, right? But secretly we work together. Get weekends off, we can even live together."

Coyul bowed to her improvisation. "Sherry, you improve on the masters."

"That's just the beginning. Gifts from the gods: we could introduce pizza."

Coyul's approval curdled slightly, but Scheherazade missed it.

Lance felt a bit giddy. He'd always wanted to be a hero and made it in his death. This was the next giant step. A messiah. An eternal good guy. "I'll do it."

"Right on. We got it knocked." Scheherazade gave him a long, deep kiss.

"What—" Lance's blood pressure took a moment to subside. "What should I be, Protestant or Catholic?"

It was Coyul's professional opinion that he should start simple and see which way the wind blew. There were built-in advantages. "Think of the theological development you'll save them. The women will love you. The men will love you. You might just skip the Dark Ages altogether, blending into one redemptive and thoroughly sexy godhead. Purji, I salute your genius." He blew her a kiss.

"And I, darling. Yours the seed."

"Lancelance*lance,* come on! Talk about significance. Stars are being born." Scheherazade took his face in tender hands. "And listen, lover: you can *die* for them. Over and over."

"A perennial favorite, never outsold," Coyul noted. "The Golden Bough never had it so good." He gestured with a flourish to Purji. "My trained and courteous assistant will handle the details of passage."

A heady moment while Lance's imagination went into overdrive, smoldered with each new possibility, roared into flame with the notion of death and martyrdom not only hallowed but painless and recyclable. In one cinematic vision, he saw Scheherazade pursued by bigoted males, bruised and bleeding, cornered against a wall, only to be saved by himself. Let him who is without sin . . . Followed by disciples, speaking in parables, performing miracles. He saw himself on the Cross, forgiving them for not knowing what they did, blessing them even in his agony, and then coming home to Sherry after a hard but satisfying day.

"Sherry, it's big."

"The biggest," she breathed. "What are we waiting for? Can we go now?"

"Come as you are," Purji beckoned. "You won't need anything. The ship is waiting. Coyul, dear, I'll just drop off the children on Keljia. Don't be too radical before I get back. Low profile."

He crossed his heart. "Death Valley."

"Thank you, sir. I'll make a good messiah." Lance started after Scheherazade but halted in the doorway with a major consideration. "Shouldn't there be a devil?"

"Oh no, don't even think of it," Coyul quashed the notion firmly. "Trust me, the Keljians will create one of their own."

"Are you sure?"

"Look what they did to me. Who wants to believe he's a bastard without help? *Au revoir.*"

"You let your hair grow," Scheherazade advised Lance as they went, "and I'll get some serious white underwear. From now on we think image. This is a com*mit*ment."

"Back soon, dear." With a wave, Purji vanished after the godlings.

"Drive carefully."

Alone, Coyul pondered aloud to the empty room: "What hath God wrought?"

He hoped the rest of the day might be as inspired as the beginning, but that would be rank optimism. A libation was in order. Coyul scanned the Candor-Ginsberg shelves and fridge, finding only a wasteland of diet soft drinks. He materialized a Glen Morangie on the rocks and sipped appreciatively, gradually aware of another voice in the room, soft but febrile with excitement.

". . . sex and redemption in one package. Yeah!" A pleased chortle. "Why didn't *I* think of that? Psst—hey, Prince?"

Coyul looked around. "Who's there?"

"Over here. The answering machine."

"Oh, it's you. How are you getting on?"

"Bored, man. How long do I have to stay a machine?"

Coyul's mind was elsewhere. "Refresh me. What did you do?"

"Nothing," the machine protested innocently. "Just free enterprise. I started a popular religion."

Coyul finished his drink, frowning. "So you did. A very lucrative one."

"So did Rome. Did you hang this kind of rap on Saint Paul? How *long?*"

"Don't call me. I'll call you."

"Hey—there he is!" The camera crew charged into the room through the open door, Cathy Cataton in the lead, adjusting her microphone. "Sorry to be a drag, Prince, but you're news again. Quick with the lights, guys. Stand over here, Coyul."

The Prince was startled out of his composure. "What . . . what the hell is this?"

"Makeup, check me out."

A small ferret of a woman writhed between Cataton and Coyul, inspecting the telereporter's makeup, patting it with a cotton swab. Another technician relieved Coyul of his drink. "Not on camera, sir."

"I repeat: what the hell is going on?"

"You're being sued," Cataton informed him with a spritely grin. "Any reaction on that? Ready? Okay, we're live."

No reaction but shock. While Coyul tried to avoid the microphone aimed at him, a large, florid man filled the doorway. Coyul recognized Reverend Arlen Strutley, recently fallen from Grace but spectacularly repented in front of a million TV viewers. Strutley fixed Coyul with a baleful eye, brandishing a folded paper. Behind him, more of the faithful jostled to get into the room.

"Prince of Darkness! Sower of discord. I have here a summons."

"Strutley, didn't they bust you?"

Strutley darkened with offense. "My confession was televised. The charges against me were blown out of all proportion."

And to prove the point, the cry went up from his adoring claque: "THREE CHEERS FOR REVEREND STRUTLEY."

"Redeemed through media. You wept prettily," Coyul admired.

"Oh, you creature of the dark." Strutley's voice broke with the best-known sob on television. "Come to judgment. Here." He thrust the paper at Coyul. The word SUMMONS was prominent in Gothic type. "We, the Christian League for an Orthodox Topside—"

"Good old CLOT." Coyul pocketed the summons; what else was new?

"—are suing you for gross misuse of office."

"In fully televised hearing." Cataton leaned into camera shot. "Stay tuned. BSTV will not carry this."

Reverend Strutley began to perspire profusely. He didn't really have to, but it made for an impassioned image. If he knew anything, Strutley knew ratings and his flock. "For outright fraud in presenting a false *Je*sus. Trial convenes in a week."

Cataton's mike jabbed at Coyul. "Will it be no contest or will you go to trial?"

"No comment, not without counsel." Coyul glanced at the summons. The charges were fulsome.

"But can you tell the viewers who'll defend you?"

"No. I don't know. This is all too—" *Speed, where the hell are you?*

"Cringe, Satan," Strutley trumpeted. "Cringe before JUSTICE!"

"Lay-ance!"

The new voice overrode even Strutley's stentorian lung power, the hunting cry of a jilted assassin. "Lay-ance, you sunva*betch!*" Into the already crowded room speared a flying wedge of robust females, Letti Candor their point. Technicians were shouldered out of the way as Letti hewed her path to the center of the room. "Where is mah husband? He *can't* desert me."

"Rejoice," Coyul informed her. "He is risen."

"You!" Letti's arm snapped out like a switchblade. "The Devil—get him!"

Letti launched herself at Coyul with a banshee yell, a killing machine. Her attack triggered a domino effect. Coyul went down, toppling Reverend Strutley. Several of Letti's more nearsighted friends, geared for blood and not at all selective, mistook the reverend for Coyul and fell on him like demented soldier ants.

"Speed," Coyul wailed as Letti's nails tore a tiger-swath through his face and a swatch of fine shirting. "Someone get Josh Speed—stop this at once, Mrs. Candor. I'm becoming quite put out. SPEEEED!"

Letti went for the jugular. "SUNVABETCH."

"Oh, hell," Coyul muttered. "Always something." He relapsed to pure light form, ground zero at Hiroshima. Blind as a rabbit in a high-beam headlight, Letti groped for something to rend. "Where's he at? Where'd that old Devil go?"

"Can't see a thing," complained Bernice, doing mayhem on Strutley by Braille, "but I got something here."

The remains of Reverend Strutley could no longer remonstrate. Blind as the rest of them, but in journalistic clover, Cathy Cataton stumbled to one side, a wounded but gallant chief still at the helm. "Beautiful! And we're exclusive. Benny, what's happening?"

"Who knows?" he hooted, blind and joyous as Cataton, "but they're doing it good."

"Keep rolling." Cataton leaned against the wall in utter contentment. "It is Heaven, it is the promised land. I love it. I *love* it."

ABOUT THE AUTHOR
An Apology

[PARKE GODWIN has been repeatedly warned by the Publisher to put the comedy *in* the book, not after it in biographical material, which should be dignified and factual. He has been frequently reminded that SF/fantasy is a genre of noble mien and purpose, blessed with mature, dedicated artists and discriminating readers; that he stepped from poor taste to *lèse-majesté* in characterizing several contemporary masters of fantasy as needing "a stiff drink, a roll in the hay, and a long blue pencil," or his own hardworking editor as a fugitive sled dog. As of the present volume, the Publisher served notice that no more of this questionable levity would be countenanced. Accordingly, the Author submitted the following biographical notes, which he maintains are completely factual. —ED.]

Born: Harold Parke Godwin, Brooklyn, NY 1/28/29. Blood: O-pos. No allergies. No religious affil.

Education: Unimpressive. No degree. Once failed Lunch.

Marital Status: Divorced since 1968. Instinctive bachelor.

Politics: Liberal Democrat. Always regarded with suspicion by Republican aunt in Scarsdale.

Passions: Music and theater, good prose, good comedy, good friends, good cooking, poker.

Dislikes: Evangelists and airline food, yuppies, writers who spend more time at conventions than work.

Regrets: As a young man, ignored many chances to be kind. Once voted for Eisenhower.

Disposition: Not misanthropic but solitary. Articulate as hell when drunk but tends to fall down. Given to nostalgia for lost things like America. Would like her back when she gets over Falwell, North and other agonized patriots. Tends to laugh over things that make him weep, like his country, because no one wants to listen to a middle-aged writer soap-box his audience into troubled sleep.

Salient Faults: Quick temper as quickly cooled. Occasionally caustic, sometimes given to snap judgments and lecturing of friends on what's good for them, but improving with age.

Work Habits: Messy. Writes longhand, paces, mumbles, chain-smokes. Revises endlessly on an Italian typewriter that resembles a Polish joke. Worries over structure; a crashing bore on the subject of tightness. Clumsy, the natural prey of mechanical devices and typewriter ribbons.

Current: Recently moved from Manhattan to California. A dog fancier all his life, has found two cats, one stoic and the other mad, that he actually likes.